PENGUIN BOOKS

THE BELLAROSA CONNECTION

Saul Bellow was awarded the Nobel Prize for Literature in 1976. His novel *Humboldt's Gift* won the Pulitzer Prize the previous year. He is the only novelist to receive three National Book Awards, for *The Adventures of Augie March*; *Herzog*; and *Mr. Sammler's Planet*. *The Bellarosa Connection* is his fifteenth book.

THE
BELLAROSA
CONNECTION

SAUL BELLOW

PENGUIN BOOKS

PENGUIN BOOKS

Published by the Penguin Group

Viking Penguin, a division of Penguin Books USA Inc.,

40 West 23rd Street, New York, New York 10010, U.S.A.

Penguin Books Ltd, 27 Wrights Lane, London W8 5TZ, England

Penguin Books Australia Ltd, Ringwood, Victoria, Australia

Penguin Books Canada Ltd, 2801 John Street,

Markham, Ontario, Canada L3R 1B4

Penguin Books (N.Z.) Ltd, 182–190 Wairau Road,

Auckland 10, New Zealand

Penguin Books Ltd, Registered Offices:

Harmondsworth, Middlesex, England

First published in Penguin Books 1989

1 3 5 7 9 10 8 6 4 2

LIBRARY OF CONGRESS CATALOGING IN PUBLICATION DATA

Bellow, Saul.

The bellarosa connection / Saul Bellow.

p.   cm.

ISBN 0 14 01.2686 4

I. Title.

PS3503.E4488B45 1989

813'.52—dc20   89–32936

Printed in the United States of America

Set in Melior

Designed by Michael Ian Kaye

To my dear friend
John Auerbach

THE
BELLAROSA
CONNECTION

As founder of the Mnemosyne Institute in Philadelphia, forty years in the trade, I trained many executives, politicians, and members of the defense establishment, and now that I am retired, with the Institute in the capable hands of my son, I would like to *forget* about remembering. Which is an Alice-in-Wonderland proposition. In your twilight years, having hung up your gloves (or sheathed your knife), you don't want to keep doing what you did throughout your life: a change, a change—your kingdom for a change! A lawyer will walk away from his clients, a doctor from his patients, a general will paint china, a diplomatist turn to fly fishing. My case is different in that I owe my worldly success to the innate gift of memory—a tricky word, "innate," referring to the hidden sources of everything that really matters. As I used to say to clients, "Memory is life." That was a neat way to impress a member of the National Security Council whom I was coaching, but it puts me now in an uncomfortable position because if you have worked in memory, which is life itself, there is no retirement except in death.

There are other discomforts to reckon with: This gift of mine became the foundation of a commercial success—an income from X millions soundly invested and an antebellum house in Philadelphia furnished by my late wife, a woman who knew everything there was to know about eighteenth-century furniture. Since I am not one of your stubborn defensive rationalizers who deny that they misuse their talents and insist that they can face God with a clear conscience, I force myself to remember that I was not born in a Philadelphia house with twenty-foot ceilings but began life as the child of Russian Jews from New Jersey. A walking memory file like me can't trash his beginnings or distort his early history. Sure, in the universal process of self-revision anybody can be carried away from the true facts. For

2

instance, Europeanized Americans in Europe will assume a false English or French correctness and bring a disturbing edge of self-consciousness into their relations with their friends. I have observed this. It makes an unpleasant impression. So whenever I was tempted to fake it, I asked myself, "And how are things out in New Jersey?"

The matters that concern me now had their moving axis in New Jersey. These are not data from the memory bank of a computer. I am preoccupied with feelings and longings, and emotional memory is nothing like rocketry or gross national products. What we have before us are the late Harry Fonstein and his late wife, Sorella. My pictures of them are probably too clear and pleasing to be true. Therefore they have to be represented pictorially first and then *wiped out and reconstituted*. But these are technical considerations, having to do with the difference between literal and affective recollection.

If you were living in a house of such dimensions, among armoires, hangings, Persian rugs, sideboards, carved fireplaces, ornamented ceilings—with a closed garden and a bathtub on a marble dais fitted with a faucet that would not be out of place in the Trevi Fountain—you would better understand why the recollection of a refugee like Fonstein and his Newark wife might become significant.

No, he, Fonstein, wasn't a poor schlepp; he succeeded in business and made a fair amount of dough. Nothing like my Philadelphia millions, but not bad for a guy who arrived after the war via Cuba and got a late start in the heating business—and, moreover, a gimpy Ga-

3

litzianer. Fonstein wore an orthopedic shoe, and there were other peculiarities: His hair looked thin, but it was anything but weak, it was a strong black growth, and although sparse it was vividly kinky. The head itself was heavy enough to topple a less determined man. His eyes were dark and they were warm, so perhaps it was their placement that made them look shrewd as well. Perhaps it was the expression of his mouth—not severe, not even unkind—which worked together with the dark eyes. You got a smart inspection from this immigrant.

We were not related by blood. Fonstein was the nephew of my stepmother, whom I called Aunt Mildred (a euphemistic courtesy—I was far too old for mothering when my widower father married her). Most of Fonstein's family were killed by the Germans. In Auschwitz he would have been gassed immediately, because of the orthopedic boot. Some Dr. Mengele would have pointed his swagger stick to the left, and Fonstein's boot might by now have been on view in the camp's exhibition hall—they have a hill of cripple boots there, and a hill of crutches and of back braces and one of human hair and one of eyeglasses. Objects that might have been useful in German hospitals or homes.

Harry Fonstein and his mother, Aunt Mildred's sister, had escaped from Poland. Somehow they had reached Italy. In Ravenna there were refugee relatives, who helped as well as they could. The heat was on Italian Jews too, since Mussolini had adopted the Nuremberg racial laws. Fonstein's mother, who was a diabetic, soon died, and Fonstein went on to Milan, traveling with phony papers while learning Italian as fast as he was able. My father, who had a passion for refugee stories, told me all this. He hoped it would straighten me out to hear what people had suffered in Europe, in the real world.

"I want you to see Mildred's nephew," my old man said to me in Lakewood, New Jersey, about forty years ago. "Just a young fellow, maybe younger than you. Got away from the Nazis, dragging one foot. He's just off the boat from Cuba. Not long married."

I was at the bar of paternal judgment again, charged with American puerility. When would I shape up, at last! At the age of thirty-two, I still behaved like a twelve-year-old, hanging out in Greenwich Village, immature, drifting, a layabout, shacking up with Bennington girls, a foolish intellectual gossip, nothing in his head but froth—the founder, said my father with comic bewilderment, of the Mnemosyne Institute, about as profitable as it was pronounceable.

As my Village pals liked to say, it cost no more than twelve hundred dollars a year to be poor—or to play at poverty, yet another American game.

Surviving-Fonstein, with all the furies of Europe at his back, made me look bad. But he wasn't to blame for that, and his presence actually made my visits easier. It was only on the odd Sunday that I paid my respects to the folks at home in green Lakewood, near Lakehurst, where in the thirties the Graf Hindenburg Zeppelin had gone up in flames as it approached its fatal mooring mast, and the screams of the dying could be heard on the ground.

Fonstein and I took turns at the chessboard with my

father, who easily beat us both—listless competitors who had the architectural weight of Sunday on our caryatid heads. Sorella Fonstein sometimes sat on the sofa, which had a transparent zippered plastic cover. Sorella was a New Jersey girl—correction: lady. She was very heavy and she wore makeup. Her cheeks were downy. Her hair was done up in a beehive. A pince-nez, highly unusual, a deliberate disguise, gave her a theatrical air. She was still a novice then, trying on these props. Her aim was to achieve an authoritative, declarative manner. However, she was no fool.

Fonstein's place of origin was Lemberg, I think. I wish I had more patience with maps. I can visualize continents and the outlines of countries, but I'm antsy about exact locations. Lemberg is now Lvov, as Danzig is Gdansk. I never was strong in geography. My main investment was in memory. As an undergraduate showing off at parties, I would store up and reel off lists of words fired at me by a circle of twenty people. Hence I can tell you more than you will want to know about Fonstein. In 1938 his father, a jeweler, didn't survive the confiscation by the Germans of his investments (valuable property) in Vienna. When the war had broken out, with Nazi paratroopers dressed as nuns spilling from planes, Fonstein's sister and her husband hid in the countryside, and both were caught and ended in the camps. Fonstein and his mother escaped to Zagreb and eventually got to Ravenna. It was in the north of Italy that Mrs. Fonstein died, and she was buried in a Jewish cemetery, perhaps the Venetian one. Then and there Fonstein's adolescence came to an end. A refugee with an orthopedic boot, he had to consider his moves carefully. "He couldn't vault over walls like Douglas Fairbanks," said Sorella.

I could see why my father took to Fonstein. Fonstein had survived the greatest ordeal of Jewish history. He still looked as if the worst, even now, would not take him by surprise. The impression he gave was unusually firm. When he spoke to you he engaged your look and held it. This didn't encourage small talk. Still, there were hints of wit at the corners of his mouth and around the eyes. So you didn't want to play the fool with Fonstein. I sized him up as a Central European Jewish type. He saw me, probably, as an immature unstable Jewish American, humanly ignorant and loosely kind: in the history of civilization, something new in the way of human types, perhaps not so bad as it looked at first.

To survive in Milan he had to learn Italian pretty damn quick. So as not to waste time, he tried to arrange to speak it even in his dreams. Later, in Cuba, he acquired Spanish too. He was gifted that way. In New Jersey he soon was fluent in English, though to humor me he spoke Yiddish now and then; it was the right language for his European experiences. I had had a tame war myself—company clerk in the Aleutians. So I listened, stooped over him (like a bishop's crook; I had six or eight inches on him), for he was the one who had seen real action.

In Milan he did kitchen work, and in Turin he was a hall porter and shined shoes. By the time he got to Rome he was an assistant concierge. Before long he was working on the Via Veneto. The city was full of Germans, and as Fonstein's German was good, he was employed as an interpreter now and then. He was noticed by Count Ciano, Mussolini's son-in-law and foreign minister.

"So you knew him?"

"Yes, but he didn't know me, not by name. When he gave a party and needed extra translators, I was sent for. There was a reception for Hitler—"

"You mean you saw Hitler?"

"My little boy says it that way too: 'My daddy saw Adolf Hitler.' Hitler was at the far end of the *grande salle*."

"Did he give a speech?"

"Thank God I wasn't close by. Maybe he made a statement. He ate some pastry. He was in military uniform."

"Yes, I've seen pictures of him on company manners, acting sweet."

"One thing," said Fonstein. "There was no color in his face."

"He wasn't killing anybody that day."

"There was nobody he couldn't kill if he liked, but this was a reception. I was happy he didn't notice me."

"I think I would have been grateful too," I said. "You can even feel love for somebody who can kill you but doesn't. Horrible love, but it is a kind of love."

"He would have gotten around to me. My trouble began with this reception. A police check was run, my papers were fishy, and that's why I was arrested."

My father, absorbed in his knights and rooks, didn't look up, but Sorella Fonstein, sitting in state as obese ladies seem to do, took off her pince-nez (she had been copying a recipe) and said, probably because her husband needed help at this point in his story, "He was locked up."

"Yes, I see."

"You *can't* see," said my stepmother. "Nobody could guess who saved him."

Sorella, who had been a teacher in the Newark school system, made a teacherly gesture. She raised her arm as though to mark a check on the blackboard beside a student's sentence. "Here comes the strange element. This is where Billy Rose plays a part."

I said, "Billy Rose, in Rome? What would he be doing there? Are we talking about Broadway Billy Rose? You mean Damon Runyon's pal, the guy who married Fanny Brice?"

"He can't believe it," said my stepmother.

In Fascist Rome, the child of her sister, her own flesh and blood, had seen Hitler at a reception. He was put in prison. There was no hope for him. Roman Jews were then being trucked to caves outside the city and shot. But he was saved by a New York celebrity.

"You're telling me," I said, "that Billy was running an underground operation in Rome?"

"For a while, yes, he had an Italian organization," said Sorella. Just then I needed an American intermediary. The range of Aunt Mildred's English was limited. Besides, she was a dull lady, slow in all her ways, totally unlike my hasty, vivid father. Mildred had a powdered look, like her own strudel. Her strudel was the best.

But when she talked to you she lowered her head. She too had a heavy head. You saw her parted hair oftener than her face.

"Billy Rose did good things too," she said, nursing her fingers in her lap. On Sundays she wore a green, beaded dark dress.

"*That* character! I can't feature it. The Aquacade man? He saved you from the Roman cops?"

"From the Nazis." My stepmother again lowered her head when she spoke. It was her dyed and parted hair that I had to interpret.

"How did you find this out?" I asked Fonstein.

"I was in a cell by myself. Those years, every jail in Europe was full, I guess. Then one day, a stranger showed up and talked to me through the grille. You know what? I thought maybe Ciano sent him. It came in my mind because this Ciano could have asked for me at the hotel. Sure he dressed in fancy uniforms and walked around with his hand on a long knife he carried in his belt. He was a playactor, but I thought he was civilized. He was pleasant. So when the man stood by the grille and looked at me, I went over and said, 'Ciano?' He shook one finger back and forth and said, 'Billy Rose.' I had no idea what he meant. Was it one word or two? A man or a woman? The message from this Italianer was: 'Tomorrow night, same time, your door will be open. Go out in the corridor. Keep turning left. And nobody will stop you. A person will be waiting in a car, and he'll take you to the train for Genoa.' "

"Why, that little operator! Billy had an underground

all to himself," I said. "He must've seen Leslie Howard in *The Scarlet Pimpernel*."

"Next night, the guard didn't lock my door after supper, and when the corridor was empty I came out. I felt as if I had whiskey in my legs, but I realized they were holding me for deportation, the SS was at work already, so I opened every door, walked upstairs, downstairs, and when I got to the street there was a car waiting and people leaning on it, speaking in normal voices. When I came up, the driver pushed me in the back and drove me to the Trastevere station. He gave me new identity papers. He said nobody would be looking for me, because my whole police file had been stolen. There was a hat and coat for me in the rear seat, and he gave me the name of a hotel in Genoa, by the waterfront. That's where I was contacted. I had passage on a Swedish ship to Lisbon."

Europe could go to hell without Fonstein.

My father looked at us sidelong with those keen eyes of his. He had heard the story many times.

I came to know it too. I got it in episodes, like a Hollywood serial—the Saturday thriller, featuring Harry Fonstein and Billy Rose, or Bellarosa. For Fonstein, in Genoa, while he was hiding in great fear in a waterfront hotel, had no other name for him. During the voyage, nobody on the refugee ship had ever heard of Bellarosa.

When the ladies were in the kitchen and my father was in the den, reading the Sunday paper, I would ask Fonstein for further details of his adventures (his torments). He couldn't have known what mental files they were going into or that they were being cross-referenced with Billy Rose—one of those insignificant-significant characters whose name will be recognized chiefly by show-biz historians. The late Billy, the business partner of Prohibition hoodlums, the sidekick of Arnold Rothstein; multimillionaire Billy, the protégé of Bernard Baruch, the young shorthand prodigy whom Woodrow Wilson, mad for shorthand, invited to the White House for a discussion of the rival systems of Pitman and Gregg; Billy the producer, the consort of Eleanor Holm, the mermaid queen of the New York World's Fair; Billy the collector of Matisse, Seurat, and so forth . . . nationally syndicated Billy, the gossip columnist. A Village pal of mine was a member of his ghostwriting team.

This was the Billy to whom Harry Fonstein owed his life.

I spoke of this ghostwriter—Wolfe was his name—and thereafter Fonstein may have considered me a possible channel to Billy himself. He never had met Billy, you see. Apparently Billy refused to be thanked by the Jews his Broadway underground had rescued.

The Italian agents who had moved Fonstein from place to place wouldn't talk. The Genoa man referred to Bellarosa but answered none of Fonstein's questions. I assume that Mafia people from Brooklyn had put together Billy's Italian operation. After the war, Sicilian gangsters were decorated by the British for their work in the Resistance. Fonstein said that with Italians, when they had secrets to keep, tiny muscles came out in the face that nobody otherwise saw. "The man lifted up his hands as if he was going to steal a shadow off the wall and stick it in his pocket." Yesterday a hit man, today working against the Nazis.

Fonstein's type was *edel*—well-bred—but he also was a tough Jew. Sometimes his look was that of a man holding the lead in the hundred-meter breast-stroke race. Unless you shot him, he was going to win. He had something in common with his Mafia saviors, whose secrets convulsed their faces.

During the crossing he thought a great deal about the person who had had him smuggled out of Italy, imagining various kinds of philanthropists and idealists ready to spend their last buck to rescue their people from Treblinka.

"How was I supposed to guess what kind of man—or maybe a committee, the Bellarosa Society—did it?"

No, it was Billy acting alone on a spurt of feeling for his fellow Jews and squaring himself to outwit Hitler and Himmler and cheat them of their victims. On another day he'd set his heart on a baked potato, a hot dog, a cruise around Manhattan on the Circle Line. There were, however, spots of deep feeling in flimsy Billy. The God of his fathers still mattered. Billy was as spattered as a Jackson Pollock painting, and among the main trickles was his Jewishness, with other streaks flowing toward secrecy—streaks of sexual weakness, sexual humiliation. At the same time, he had to have his name in the paper. As someone said, he had a bug-like tropism for publicity. Yet his rescue operation in Europe remained secret.

Fonstein, one of the refugee crowd sailing to New

York, wondered how many others among the passengers might have been saved by Billy. Nobody talked much. Experienced people begin at a certain point to keep their own counsel and refrain from telling their stories to one another. Fonstein was eaten alive by his fantasies of what he would do in New York. He said that at night when the ship rolled he was like a weighted rope, twisting and untwisting. He expected that Billy, if he had saved scads of people, would have laid plans for their future too. Fonstein didn't foresee that they would gather together and cry like Joseph and his brethren. Nothing like that. No, they would be put up in hotels or maybe in an old sanitarium, or boarded with charitable families. Some would want to go to Palestine; most would opt for the U.S.A. and study English, perhaps finding jobs in industry or going to technical schools.

But Fonstein was detained at Ellis Island. Refugees were not being admitted then. "They fed us well," he told me. "I slept in a wire bin, on an upper bunk. I could see Manhattan. They told me, though, that I'd have to go to Cuba. I still didn't know who Billy was, but I waited for his help.

"And after a few weeks a woman was sent by Rose Productions to talk to me. She dressed like a young girl—lipstick, high heels, earrings, a hat. She had legs like posts and looked like an actress from the Yiddish theater, about ready to begin to play older roles, disappointed and sad. She called herself a *dramatisten* and was in her fifties if not more. She said my case was being turned over to the Hebrew Immigrant Aid Society. They would take care of me. No more Billy Rose."

"You must have been shook up."

"Of course. But I was even more curious than dashed. I asked her about the man who rescued me. I said I would like to give Billy my thanks personally. She brushed this aside. Irrelevant. She said, 'After Cuba, maybe.' I saw that she doubted it would happen. I asked, did he help lots of people. She said, 'Sure he helps, but himself he helps first, and you should hear him scream over a dime.' He was very famous, he was rich, he owned the Ziegfeld building and was continually in the papers. What was he like? Tiny, greedy, smart. He underpaid the employees, and they were afraid of the boss. He dressed very well, and he was a Broadway character and sat all night in cafés. 'He can call up Governor Dewey and talk to him whenever he likes.'

"That was what she said. She said also, 'He pays me twenty-two bucks, and if I even hint a raise I'll be fired. So what then? Second Avenue is dead. For Yiddish radio there's a talent oversupply. If not for the boss, I'd fade away in the Bronx. Like this, at least I work on Broadway. But you're a greener, and to you it's all a blank.'

" 'If he hadn't saved me from deportation, I'd have ended like others in my family. I owe him my life.' "

" 'Probably so,' she agreed.

" 'Wouldn't it be normal to be interested in a man you did that for? Or at least have a look, shake a hand, speak a word?'

" 'It would have *been* normal,' she said. 'Once.'

"I began to realize," said Fonstein, "that she was a sick person. I believe she had TB. It wasn't the face powder that made her so white. White was to her what yellow color is to a lemon. What I saw was not makeup—it was the Angel of Death. Tubercular people often are quick and nervous. Her name was Missus Hamet—*khomet* being the Yiddish word for a horse collar. She was from Galicia, like me. We had the same accent."

A Chinese singsong. Aunt Mildred had it too—comical to other Jews, uproarious in a Yiddish music hall.

" 'HIAS will get work for you in Cuba. They take terrific care of you fellas. Billy thinks the war is in a new stage. Roosevelt is for King Saud, and those Arabians hate Jews and keep the door to Palestine shut. That's why Rose changed his operations. He and his friends are now chartering ships for refugees. The Rumanian government will sell them to the Jews at fifty bucks a head, and there are seventy thousand of them. That's a lot of moola. Better hurry before the Nazis take over Rumania.' "

Fonstein said very reasonably, "I told her how useful I might be. I spoke four languages. But she was hardened to people pleading, ingratiating themselves with their lousy gratitude. Hey, it's an ancient routine," said Fonstein, standing on the four-inch sole of his laced boot. His hands were in his pockets and took no part in the eloquence of his shrug. His face was, briefly, like a notable face in a museum case, in a dark room, its pallor spotlighted so that the skin was stippled, a curious ef-

16

fect, like stony gooseflesh. Except that he was not on show for the brilliant deeds he had done. As men go, he was as plain as seltzer.

Billy didn't want his gratitude. First your suppliant takes you by the knees. Then he asks for a small loan. He wants a handout, a pair of pants, a pad to sleep in, a meal ticket, a bit of capital to go into business. One man's gratitude is poison to his benefactor. Besides, Billy was fastidious about persons. In principle they were welcome to his goodwill, but they drove him to hysteria when they put their moves on him.

"Never having set foot in Manhattan, I had no clue," said Fonstein. "Instead there were bizarre fantasies, but what good were those? New York is a collective fantasy of millions. There's just so much a single mind can do with it."

Mrs. Horsecollar (her people had had to be low-caste teamsters in the Old Country) warned Fonstein, "Billy doesn't want you to mention his name to HIAS."

"So how did I get to Ellis Island?"

"Make up what you like. Say that a married Italian woman loved you and stole money from her husband to buy papers for you. But no leaks on Billy."

Here my father told Fonstein, "I can mate you in five moves." My old man would have made a mathematician if he had been more withdrawn from human affairs. Only, his motive for concentrated thought was winning. My father wouldn't apply himself where there was no opponent to beat.

I have my own fashion of testing my powers. Memory is my field. But also my faculties are not what they once

17

were. I haven't got Alzheimer's, *absit omen* or *nicht da gedacht*—no sticky matter on my recollection cells. But I am growing slower. Now who was the man that Fonstein had worked for in Havana? Once I had instant retrieval for such names. No electronic system was in it with me. Today I darken and grope occasionally. But thank God I get a reprieve—Fonstein's Cuban employer was Salkind, and Fonstein was his legman. All over South America there were Yiddish newspapers. In the Western Hemisphere, Jews were searching for surviving relatives and studying the published lists of names. Many DPs were dumped in the Caribbean and in Mexico. Fonstein quickly added Spanish and English to his Polish, German, Italian, and Yiddish. He took engineering courses in a night school instead of hanging out in bars or refugee cafés. To tourists, Havana was a holiday town for gambling, drinking, and whoring—an abortion center as well. Unhappy single girls came down from the States to end their love pregnancies. Others, more farsighted, flew in to look among the refugees for husbands and wives. Find a spouse of a stable European background, a person schooled in suffering and endurance. Somebody who had escaped death. Women who found no takers in Baltimore, Kansas City, or Minneapolis, worthy girls to whom men never proposed, found husbands in Mexico, Honduras, and Cuba.

After five years, Fonstein's employer was prepared to vouch for him, and sent for Sorella, his niece. To imagine what Fonstein and Sorella saw in each other when they were introduced was in the early years beyond me. Whenever we met in Lakewood, Sorella was dressed in a suit. When she crossed her legs and he noted the volume of her underthighs, an American observer like me could, and would, picture the entire woman unclothed, and depending on his experience of life and his acquaintance with art, he might attribute her type to an appropriate painter. In my mental picture of Sorella I chose Rembrandt's Saskia over the nudes of Rubens. But then Fonstein, when he took off his surgical boot, was . . . well, he had imperfections too. So man and wife could forgive each other. I think my tastes would have been more like those of Billy Rose—water nymphs, Loreleis, or chorus girls. Eastern European men had more sober standards. In my father's place, I would have had to make the sign of the cross over Aunt Mildred's face while getting into bed with her—something exorcistic (farfetched) to take the curse off. But you see, I was not my father, I was his spoiled American son. Your stoical forebears took their lumps in bed. As for Billy, with his trousers and shorts at his ankles, chasing girls who had come to be auditioned, he would have done better with Mrs. Horsecollar. If he'd forgive her bagpipe udders and estuary leg veins, she'd forgive his unheroic privates, and they could pool their wretched mortalities and stand by each other for better or worse.

Sorella's obesity, her beehive coif, the preposterous pince-nez—a "lady" put-on—made me wonder: What *is* it with such people? Are they female impersonators, drag queens?

This was a false conclusion reached by a middle-class boy who considered himself an enlightened bohemian.

I was steeped in the exciting sophistication of the Village.

I was altogether wrong, dead wrong about Sorella, but at the time my perverse theory found some support in Fonstein's story of his adventures. He told me how he had sailed from New York and gone to work for Salkind in Havana while learning Spanish together with English and studying refrigeration and heating in a night school. "Till I met an American girl, down there on a visit."

"You met Sorella. And you fell in love with her?"

He gave me a hard-edged Jewish look when I spoke of love. How do you distinguish among love, need, and prudence?

Deeply experienced people—this continually impresses me—will keep things to themselves. Which is all right for those who don't intend to go beyond experience. But Fonstein belonged to an even more advanced category, those who don't put such restraints on themselves and feel able to enter the next zone; in that next zone, their aim is to convert weaknesses and secrets into burnable energy. A first-class man subsists on the matter he destroys, just as the stars do. But I am going beyond Fonstein, needlessly digressing. Sorella wanted a husband, while Fonstein needed U.S. naturalization papers. *Mariage de convenance* was how I saw it.

It's always the falsest formulation that you're proudest of.

Fonstein took a job in a New Jersey shop that subcontracted the manufacture of parts in the heating-equipment line. He did well there, a beaver for work, and made rapid progress in his sixth language. Before long he was driving a new Pontiac. Aunt Mildred said it was a wedding present from Sorella's family. "They are *so* relieved," Mildred told me. "A few years more, and Sorella would be too old for a baby." One child was what the Fonsteins had, a son, Gilbert. He was said to be a prodigy in mathematics and physics. Some years down the line, Fonstein consulted me about the boy's education. By then he had the money to send him to the best schools. Fonstein had improved and patented a thermostat, and with Sorella's indispensable help he became a rich man. She was a tiger wife. Without her, he was to tell me, there would have been no patent. "My company would have stolen me blind. I wouldn't be the man you're looking at today."

I then examined the Fonstein who stood before me. He was wearing an Italian shirt, a French necktie, and his orthopedic boot was British-made—bespoke on Jermyn Street. With that heel he might have danced the flamenco. How different from the crude Polish article, boorishly ill-made, in which he had hobbled across Europe and escaped from prison in Rome. *That* boot, as he dodged the Nazis, he had dreaded to take off, nights, for if it had been stolen he would have been caught and killed in his short-legged nakedness. The SS would not have bothered to drive him into a cattle car.

How pleased his rescuer, Billy Rose, should have been to see the Fonstein of today: the pink, white-collared Italian shirt, the Rue de Rivoli tie, knotted under Sorella's instruction, the easy hang of the imported suit, the good color of his face, which, no longer stone white,

21

had the full planes and the color of a ripe pomegranate.

But Fonstein and Billy never actually met. Fonstein had made it his business to see Billy, but Billy was never to see Fonstein. Letters were returned. Sometimes there were accompanying messages, never once in Billy's own hand. Mr. Rose wished Harry Fonstein well but at the moment couldn't give him an appointment. When Fonstein sent Billy a check accompanied by a note of thanks and the request that the money be used for charitable purposes, it was returned without acknowledgment. Fonstein came to his office and was turned away. When he tried one day to approach Billy at Sardi's he was intercepted by one of the restaurant's personnel. You weren't allowed to molest celebrities here.

Finding his way blocked, Fonstein said to Billy in his Galician-Chinese singsong, "I came to tell you I'm one of the people you rescued in Italy." Billy turned toward the wall of his booth, and Fonstein was escorted to the street.

In the course of years, long letters were sent. "I want nothing from you, not even to shake hands, but to speak man to man for a minute."

It was Sorella, back in Lakewood, who told me this, while Fonstein and my father were sunk in a trance over the chessboard. "Rose, that special party, won't see Harry," said Sorella.

My comment was, "I break my head trying to understand why it's so important for Fonstein. He's been turned down? So he's been turned down."

"To express gratitude," said Sorella. "All he wants to say is 'Thanks.' "

"And this wild pygmy absolutely refuses."

"Behaves as if Harry Fonstein never existed."

"Why, do you suppose? Afraid of the emotions? Too Jewish a moment for him? Drags him down from his standing as a full-fledged American? What's your husband's opinion?"

"Harry thinks it's some kind of change in the descendants of immigrants in this country," said Sorella.

And I remember today what a pause this answer gave me. I myself had often wondered uncomfortably about the Americanization of the Jews. One could begin with physical differences. My father's height was five feet six inches, mine was six feet two inches. To my father, this seemed foolishly wasteful somehow. Perhaps the reason was Biblical, for King Saul, who stood head and shoulders above the others, was *verrucht*—demented and doomed. The prophet Samuel had warned Israel not to take a king, and Saul did not find favor in God's eyes. Therefore a Jew should not be unnecessarily large but rather finely made, strong but compact. The main thing was to be deft and quick-witted. That was how my father was and how he would have preferred me to be. My length was superfluous, I had too much chest and shoulders, big hands, a wide mouth, a band of black mustache, too much voice, excessive hair; the shirts that covered my trunk had too many red and gray stripes, idiotically flashy. Fools ought to come in smaller sizes. A big son was a threat, a parricide. Now Fonstein de-

23

spite his short leg was a proper man, well arranged, trim, sensible, and clever. His development was hastened by Hitlerism. Losing your father at the age of fourteen brings your childhood to an end. Burying your mother in a foreign cemetery, no time to mourn, caught with false documents, doing time in the slammer ("sitting" is the Jewish term for it: "*Er hat gesessen*"). A man acquainted with grief. No time for froth or moronic laughter, for vanities and games, for climbing the walls, for effeminacies or infantile plaintiveness.

I didn't agree, of course, with my father. We were bigger in my generation because we had better nutrition. We were, moreover, less restricted, we had wider liberties. We grew up under a larger range of influences and thoughts—we were the children of a great democracy, bred to equality, living it up with no pales to confine us. Why, until the end of the last century, the Jews of Rome were still locked in for the night; the Pope ceremonially entered the ghetto once a year and spat ritually on the garments of the Chief Rabbi. Were we giddy here? No doubt about it. But there were no cattle cars waiting to take us to camps and gas chambers.

One can think of such things—and think and *think*—but nothing is resolved by these historical meditations. To *think* doesn't settle anything. No idea is more than an imaginary potency, a mushroom cloud (destroying nothing, making nothing) rising from blinding consciousness.

And Billy Rose wasn't big; he was about the size of Peter Lorre. But oh! he was American. There was a penny-arcade jingle about Billy, the popping of shooting galleries, the rattling of pinballs, the weak human cry of the Times Square geckos, the lizard gaze of side-show freaks. To see him as he was, you have to place him against the whitewash glare of Broadway in the wee hours. But even such places have their grandees—people whose defects can be converted to seed money for enterprises. There's nothing in this country that you can't sell, nothing too weird to bring to market and found a fortune on. And once you got as much major real estate as Billy had, then it didn't matter that you were one of the human deer that came uptown from the Lower East Side to graze on greasy sandwich papers. Billy? Well, Billy had bluffed out mad giants like Robert Moses. He bought the Ziegfeld building for peanuts. He installed Eleanor Holm in a mansion and hung the walls with masterpieces. And he went on from there. They'd say in feudal Ireland that a proud man is a lovely man (Yeats's Parnell), but in glamorous New York he could be lovely because the columnists said he was—George Sokolsky, Walter Winchell, Leonard Lyons, the "Mid-night Earl"—and also Hollywood pals and leaders of nightclub society. Billy was all over the place. Why, he was even a newspaper columnist, and syndicated. True, he had ghostwriters, but he was the mastermind who made all the basic decisions and vetted every word they printed.

Fonstein was soon familiar with Billy's doings, more familiar than I ever was or cared to be. But then Billy had saved the man: took him out of prison, paid his way to Genoa, installed him in a hotel, got him passage on a neutral ship. None of this could Fonstein have

25

done for himself, and you'd never in the world hear him deny it.

"Of course," said Sorella, with gestures that only a two-hundred-pound woman can produce, because her delicacy rests on the mad overflow of her behind, "though my husband has given up on making contact, he hasn't stopped, and he can't stop being grateful. He's a dignified individual himself, but he's also a very smart man and has got to be conscious of the kind of person that saved him."

"Does it upset him? It could make him unhappy to be snatched from death by a kibitzer."

"It gets to him sometimes, yes."

She proved quite a talker, this Sorella. I began to look forward to our conversations as much for what came out of her as for the intrinsic interest of the subject. Also I had mentioned that I was a friend of Wolfe, one of Billy's ghosts, and maybe she was priming me. Wolfe might even take the matter up with Billy. I informed Sorella up front that Wolfe would never do it. "This Wolfe," I told her, "is a funny type, a little guy who seduces big girls. Very clever. He hangs out at Birdland and dotes on Broadway freaks. In addition, he's a Yale-trained intellectual heavy, or so he likes to picture himself; he treasures his kinks and loves being deep. For instance, his mother also is his cleaning lady. He told me recently as I watched a woman on her knees scrubbing out his pad, 'The old girl you're looking at is my mother.'"

"Her own dear boy?" said Sorella.

"An only child," I said.

"She must love him like anything."

"I don't doubt it for a minute. To him, that's what's deep. Although Wolfe is decent, under it all. He has to support her anyway. What harm is there in saving ten bucks a week on the cleaning? Besides which he builds up his reputation as a weirdo nihilist. He wants to become the Thomas Mann of science fiction. That's his real aim, he says, and he only dabbles in Broadway. It amuses him to write Billy's columns and break through in print with expressions like: 'I'm going to hit him on his pointy head. I'll give him such a *hit*!' "

Sorella listened and smiled, though she didn't wish to appear familiar with these underground characters and their language or habits, with Village sex or Broadway sleaze. She brought the conversation back to Fonstein's rescue and the history of the Jews.

She and I found each other congenial, and before long I was speaking as openly to her as I would in a Village conversation, let's say with Paul Goodman at the Casbah, not as though she were merely a square fat lady from the dark night of petty-bourgeois New Jersey—no more than a carrier or genetic relay to produce a science savant of the next generation. She had made a respectable ("contemptible") marriage. However, she was also a tiger wife, a tiger mother. It was no negligible person who had patented Fonstein's thermostat and rounded up the money for his little factory (it *was* little at first), meanwhile raising a boy who was a mathematical genius. She was a spirited woman, at home with ideas. This heavy tailored lady was extremely well informed. I wasn't inclined to discuss Jewish history with her—

it put my teeth on edge at first—but she overcame my resistance. She was well up on the subject, and besides, damn it, you couldn't say no to Jewish history after what had happened in Nazi Germany. You had to listen. It turned out that as the wife of a refugee she had set herself to master the subject, and I heard a great deal from her about the technics of annihilation, the large-scale-industry aspect of it. What she occasionally talked about while Fonstein and my father stared at the chessboard, sealed in their trance, was the black humor, the slapstick side of certain camp operations. Being a French teacher, she was familiar with Jarry and *Ubu Roi*, Pataphysics, Absurdism, Dada, Surrealism. Some camps were run in a burlesque style that forced you to make these connections. Prisoners were sent naked into a swamp and had to croak and hop like frogs. Children were hanged while starved, freezing slave laborers lined up on parade in front of the gallows and a prison band played Viennese light opera waltzes.

I didn't want to hear this, and I said impatiently, "All right, Billy Rose wasn't the only one in show biz. So the Germans did it too, and what they staged in Nuremberg was bigger than Billy's rally in Madison Square Garden—the 'We Will Never Die' pageant."

I understood Sorella: the object of her researches was to assist her husband. He was alive today because a little Jewish promoter took it into his queer head to organize a Hollywood-style rescue. I was invited to meditate on themes like: Can Death Be Funny? or Who Gets the Last Laugh? I wouldn't do it, though. First those people murdered you, then they forced you to brood on their crimes. It suffocated me to do this. Hunting for causes was a horrible imposition added to the original "selection," gassing, cremation. I didn't want to think of the history and psychology of these abominations, death chambers and furnaces. Stars are nuclear furnaces too. Such things are utterly beyond me, a pointless exercise.

Also my advice to Fonstein—given mentally—was: Forget it. Go American. Work at your business. Market your thermostats. Leave the theory side of it to your wife. She has a taste for it, and she's a clever woman. If she enjoys collecting a Holocaust library and wants to ponder the subject, why not? Maybe she'll write a book herself, about the Nazis and the entertainment industry. Death and mass fantasy.

My own suspicion was that there was a degree of fantasy embodied in Sorella's obesity. She was biologically dramatized in waves and scrolls of tissue. Still, she was, at bottom, a serious woman fully devoted to her husband and child. Fonstein had his talents; Sorella, however, had the business brain. And Fonstein didn't have to be told to go American. Together this couple soon passed from decent prosperity to real money. They bought property east of Princeton, off toward the ocean, they educated the boy, and when they had sent him away to camp in the summer, they traveled. Sorella, the onetime French teacher, had a taste for Europe. She had had, moreover, the good luck to find a European husband.

Toward the close of the fifties they went to Israel, and as it happened, business had brought me to Jerusalem too. The Israelis, who culturally had one of every-thing in the world, invited me to open a memory institute.

So, in the lobby of the King David, I met the Fonsteins. "Haven't seen you in years!" said Fonstein.

True, I had moved to Philadelphia and married a Main Line lady. We lived in a brownstone mansion, which had a closed garden and an 1817 staircase photographed by *American Heritage* magazine. My father had died; his widow had gone to live with a niece. I seldom saw the old lady and had to ask the Fonsteins how she was. Over the last decade I had had only one contact with the Fonsteins, a telephone conversation about their gifted boy.

This year, they had sent him to a summer camp for little science prodigies.

Sorella was particularly happy to see me. She was sitting—at her weight I suppose one generally is more comfortable seated—and she was unaffectedly pleased to find me in Jerusalem. My thought about the two of them was that it was good for a DP to have ample ballast in his missus. Besides, I believe that he loved her. My own wife was something of a Twiggy. One never does strike it absolutely right. Sorella, calling me "Cousin," said in French that she was still a *femme bien en chair*. I wondered how a man found his way among so many creases. But that was none of my business. They looked happy enough.

The Fonsteins had rented a car. Harry had relations in Haifa, and they were going to tour the north of the country. Wasn't it an extraordinary place! said Sorella, dropping her voice to a theatrical whisper. (What was there to keep secret?) Jews who were electricians and bricklayers, Jewish policemen, engineers, and sea captains. Fonstein was a good walker. In Europe he had walked a thousand miles in his Polish boot. Sorella, however, was not built for sightseeing. "I should be carried in a litter," she said. "But that's not a trade for Israelis, is it?" She invited me to have tea with her while Fonstein looked up hometown people—neighbors from Lemberg.

Before our tea, I went up to my room to read the *Herald Tribune*—one of the distinct pleasures of being abroad—but I settled down with the paper in order to think about the Fonsteins (my two-in-one habit—like using music as a background for reflection). The Fonsteins were not your predictable, disposable distant family relations who labeled themselves by their clothes, their conversation, the cars they drove, their temple memberships, their party politics. Fonstein for all his Jermyn Street boots and Italianate suits was still the man who had buried his mother in Venice and waited in his cell for Ciano to rescue him. Though his face was silent and his manner "socially advanced"— this was the only term I could apply: far from the Jewish style acquired in New Jersey communities—I believe that he was thinking intensely about his European origin and his American transformation: Part I and Part II. Signs of a tenacious memory in others seldom escape me. I always ask, however, what people are doing with their recollections. Rote, mechanical storage, an unusual capacity for retaining facts, has a limited interest for me. Idiots can have that gift. Nor do I care much for nostalgia and its associated sentiments. In most cases, I dislike it. Fonstein was *doing* something with his past. This was the lively, the active element of his still look. But you no more discussed this with a man than you asked how he felt about his smooth boot with the four-inch sole.

Then there was Sorella. No ordinary woman, she broke with every sign of ordinariness. Her obesity, assuming she had some psychic choice in the matter, was a sign of this. She might have willed herself to be thinner, for she had the strength of character to do it. Instead she accepted the challenge of size as a Houdini might have asked for tighter knots, more locks on the trunk, deeper rivers to escape from. She was, as people nowadays say, "off the continuum"—her graph went beyond the chart and filled up the whole wall. In my King David reverie, I put it that she had had to wait for an uncle in Havana to find a husband for her—she had been a matrimonial defective, a reject. To come out of it gave her a revolutionary impulse. There was going to be no sign of her early humiliation, not in *any* form, no bitter residue. What you didn't want you would shut out decisively. You had been unhealthy, lumpish. Your fat had made you pale and clumsy. Nobody, not even a lout, had come to court you. What do you do now with this painful record of disgrace? You don't bury nor do you transform it; you *annihilate* it and then use the space to draw a more powerful design. You draw it in freedom because you can afford to, not because there's anything to hide. The new design, as I saw it, was not

32

an invention. The Sorella I saw was not constructed but revealed.

I put aside the *Herald Tribune* and went down in the elevator. Sorella had settled herself on the terrace of the King David. She wore a dress of whitish beige. The bodice was ornamented with a large square of scalloped material. There was something military and also mystical about this. It made me think of the Knights of Malta—a curious thing to be associated with a Jewish lady from New Jersey. But then the medieval wall of the Old City was just across the valley. In 1959 the Israelis were still shut out of it; it was Indian country then. At the moment, I wasn't thinking of Jews and Jordanians, however. I was having a civilized tea with a huge lady who was also distinctly, authoritatively dainty. The beehive was gone. Her fair hair was cropped, she wore Turkish slippers on her small feet, which were innocently crossed under the beaten brass of the tray table. The Vale of Hinnom, once the Ottoman reservoir, was green and blossoming. What I have to say here is that I was aware of—I directly experienced—the beating of Sorella's heart as it faced the challenge of supply in so extensive an organism. This to me was a bold operation, bigger than the Turkish waterworks. I felt my own heart signifying admiration for hers—the extent of the project it had to face.

Sorella put me in a tranquil state.

"Far from Lakewood."

"That's the way travel is now," I said. "We've done something to distance. Some transformation, some bewilderment."

33

"And you've come here to set up a branch of your institute—do these people need one?"

"They think they do," I said. "They have a modified Noah's Ark idea. They don't want to miss out on anything from the advanced countries. They have to keep up with the world and be a complete microcosm."

"Do you mind if I give you a short, friendly test?"

"Go right ahead."

"Can you remember what I was wearing when we first met in your father's house?"

"You had on a gray tailored suit, not too dark, with a light stripe, and jet earrings."

"Can you tell me who built the Graf Zeppelin?"

"I can—Dr. Hugo Eckener."

"The name of your second-grade teacher, fifty years ago?"

"Miss Emma Cox."

Sorella sighed, less in admiration than in sorrow, in sympathy with the burden of so much useless information.

"That's pretty remarkable," she said. "At least your success with the Mnemosyne Institute has a legitimate basis—I wonder, do you recall the name of the woman Billy Rose sent to Ellis Island to talk to Harry?"

"That was Mrs. Hamet. Harry thought she was suffering from TB."

"Yes, that's correct."

"Why do you ask?"

"Over the years I had some contact with her. First she looked us up. Then I looked her up. I cultivated

34

her. I liked the old lady, and she found me also sympathetic. We saw a lot of each other."

"You put it all in the past tense."

"That's where it belongs. A while back, she passed away in a sanitarium near White Plains. I used to visit her. You might say a bond formed between us. She had no family to speak of. . . ."

"A Yiddish actress, wasn't she?"

"True, and she was personally theatrical, but not only from nostalgia for a vanished art—the Vilna Troupe, or Second Avenue. It was also because she had a combative personality. There was lots of sophistication in that character, lots of purpose. Plenty of patience. Plus a hell of a lot of stealth."

"What did she need the stealth for?"

"For many years she kept an eye on Billy's doings. She put everything in a journal. As well as she could, she maintained a documented file—notes on comings and goings, dated records of telephone conversations, carbon copies of letters."

"Personal or business?"

"You couldn't draw a clear line."

"What's the good of all this material?"

"I can't say exactly."

"Did she hate the man? Was she trying to get him?"

"Actually, I don't believe she was. She was very tolerant—as much as she could be, leading a nickel-and-dime life and feeling mistreated. But I don't think she wanted to nail him by his iniquities. He was a celeb, to her—that was what she called him. She ate at the

Automat; he was a celeb, so he took his meals at Sardi's, Dempsey's, or in Sherman Billingsley's joint. No hard feelings over it. The Automat gave good value for your nickels, and she used to say she had a healthier diet."

"I seem to recall she was badly treated."

"So was everybody else, and they all said they detested him. What did your friend Wolfe tell you?"

"He said that Billy had a short fuse. That he was a kind of botch. Still, it made Wolfe ecstatic to have a Broadway connection. There was glamour in the Village if you were one of Billy's ghosts. It gave Wolfe an edge with smart girls who came downtown from Vassar or Smith. He didn't have first-class intellectual credentials in the Village, he wasn't a big-time wit, but he was eager to go forward, meaning that he was prepared to take abuse—and they had plenty of it to give—from the top wise-guy theoreticians, the heavyweight pundits, in order to get an education in modern life—which meant you could combine Kierkegaard and Birdland in the same breath. He was a big chaser. But he didn't abuse or sponge on girls. When he was seducing, he started the young lady off on a box of candy. The next stage, always the same, was a cashmere sweater—both candy and cashmere from a guy who dealt in stolen goods. When the affair was over, the chicks were passed on to somebody more crude and lower on the totem pole. . . ."

Here I made a citizen's arrest, mentally—I checked myself. It was the totem pole that did it. A Jew in Jerusalem, and one who was able to explain where we were at—how Moses had handed on the law to Joshua, and Joshua to the Judges, the Judges to the Prophets, the Prophets to the Rabbis, so that at the end of the line, a Jew from secular America (a diaspora within a diaspora) could jive glibly about the swinging Village scene of the fifties and about totem poles, about Broadway lowlife and squalor. Especially if you bear in mind that this particular Jew couldn't say what place he held in this great historical procession. I had concluded long ago that the Chosen were chosen to read God's mind. Over the millennia, this turned out to be a zero-sum game.

I wasn't about to get into that.

"So old Mrs. Hamet died," I said, in a sad tone. I recalled her face as Fonstein had described it, whiter than confectioners' sugar. It was almost as though I had known her.

"She wasn't exactly a poor old thing," said Sorella. "Nobody asked her to participate, but she was a player nevertheless."

"She kept this record—why?"

"Billy obsessed her to a bizarre degree. She believed that they belonged together because they were similar—defective people. The unfit, the rejects, coming together to share each other's burden."

"Did she want to be Mrs. Rose?"

"No, no—that was out of the question. He only married celebs. She had no PR value—she was old, no figure, no complexion, no money, no status. Too late even for penicillin to save her. But she did make it her business to know everything about him. When she let herself go, she was extremely obscene. Obscenity was linked to everything. She certainly knew all the words. She could sound like a man."

"And she thought she should tell you? Share her research?"

"Me, yes. She approached us through Harry, but the friendship was with me. Those two seldom met, almost never."

"And she left you her files?"

"A journal plus supporting evidence."

"Ugh!" I said. The tea had steeped too long and was dark. Lemon lightened the color, and sugar was just what I needed late in the afternoon to pick me up. I said to Sorella, "Is this journal any good to you? You don't need any help from Billy."

"Certainly not. America, as they say, has been good to us. However, it's quite a document she left. I think you'd find it so."

"If I cared to read it."

"If you started, you'd go on, all right."

She was offering it. She had brought it with her to Jerusalem! And why had she done that? Not to show to me, certainly. She couldn't have known that she was going to meet me here. We had been out of touch for years. I was not on good terms with the family, you see. I had married a Wasp lady, and my father and I had quarreled. I was a Philadelphian now, without contacts in New Jersey. New Jersey to me was only a delay en route to New York or Boston. A psychic darkness. Whenever possible I omitted New Jersey. Anyway, I chose not to read the journal.

38

Sorella said, "You may be wondering what use I might make of it."

Well, I wondered, of course, why she hadn't left Mrs. Hamet's journal at home. Frankly, I didn't care to speculate on her motives. What I understood clearly was that she was oddly keen to have me read it. Maybe she wanted my advice. "Has your husband gone through it?" I said.

"He wouldn't understand the language."

"And it would embarrass you to translate it."

"That's more or less it," said Sorella.

"So it's pretty hairy in places? You said she knew the words. Clinical stuff didn't scare Mrs. Hamet, did it."

"In these days of scientific sex studies, there's not much that's new and shocking," said Sorella.

"The shock comes from the source. When it's someone in the public eye."

"Yes, I figured that."

Sorella was a proper person. She was not suggesting that I share any lewdnesses with her. Nothing was farther from her than evil communications. She had never in her life seduced anyone—I'd bet a year's income on that. She was as stable in character as she was immense in her person. The square on the bosom of her dress, with its scalloped design, was like a repudiation of all trivial mischief. The scallops themselves seemed to me to be a kind of message in cursive characters, warning against kinky interpretations, perverse attributions.

She was silent. She seemed to say: Do you doubt me?

Well, this was Jerusalem, and I am unusually susceptible to places. In a moment I had touched base with the Crusaders, with Caesar and Christ, the kings of Israel. There was also the heart beating in her (in me too) with the persistence of fidelity, a faith in the necessary continuation of a radical mystery—don't ask me to spell it out.

I wouldn't have felt this way in blue-collar Trenton.

Sorella was too big a person to play any kind of troublemaking games or to create minor mischief. Her eyes were like vents of atmospheric blue, and their backing (the camera obscura) referred you to the black of universal space, where there is no object to reflect the flow of invisible light.

Clarification came in a day or two, from an item in that rag the *Post*. Expected soon in Jerusalem were Billy Rose and the designer, artistic planner, and architectural sculptor Isamu Noguchi. Magnificent Rose, always a friend of Israel, was donating a sculpture garden here, filling it with his collection of masterpieces. He had persuaded Noguchi to lay it out for him—or, if that wasn't nifty enough, to preside over its creation, for Billy, as the reporter said, had the philanthropic impulses but was hopeless with the aesthetic requirements. Knew what he wanted; even more, he knew what he *didn't* want.

Any day now they would arrive. They would meet with Jerusalem planning officials, and the prime minister would invite them to dinner.

I couldn't talk to Sorella about this. The Fonsteins had gone to Haifa. Their driver would take them to Nazareth and the Galil, up to the Syrian border. Gennesaret, Capernaum, the Mount of the Beatitudes were on the itinerary. There was no need for questions; I now understood what Sorella was up to. From the poor old Hamet lady, possibly (that sapper, that mole, that dedicated researcher), she had had advance notice, and it wouldn't have been hard to learn the date of Billy's arrival with the eminent Noguchi. Sorella, if she liked, could read Billy the riot act, using Mrs. Hamet's journal as her prompt book. I wondered just how this would happen. The general intention was all I could make out. If Billy was ingenious in getting maximum attention (half magnificence, half baloney and smelling like it), if Noguchi was ingenious in the department of beautiful settings, it remained to be seen what Sorella could come up with in the way of ingenuity.

Technically, she was a housewife. On any questionnaire or application she would have put a check in the housewife box. None of what goes with that—home decoration, the choice of place mats, flatware, wallpapers, cooking utensils, the control of salt, cholesterol, carcinogens, preoccupation with hairdressers and nail care, cosmetics, shoes, dress lengths, the time devoted to shopping malls, department stores, health clubs, luncheons, cocktails—none of these things, or forces, or powers (for I see them also as powers, or even spirits), could keep a woman like Sorella in subjection. She was no more a housewife than Mrs. Hamet had been a secretary. Mrs. Hamet was a dramatic artist out of work, a tubercular, moribund, and finally demonic old woman. In leaving her dynamite journal to Sorella, she made a calculated choice, dazzlingly appropriate.

41

Since Billy and Noguchi arrived at the King David while Sorella and Fonstein were taking time off on the shore of Galilee, and although I was busy with Mnemosyne business, I nevertheless kept an eye on the newcomers as if I had been assigned by Sorella to watch and report. Predictably, Billy made a stir among the King David guests—mainly Jews from the United States. To some, it was a privilege to see a legendary personality in the lobby and the dining room, or on the terrace. For his part, he didn't encourage contacts, didn't particularly want to know anybody. He had the high color of people who are observed—the cynosure flush.

Immediately he made a scene in the pillared, carpeted lobby. El Al had lost his luggage. A messenger from the prime minister's office came to tell him that it was being traced. It might have gone on to Jakarta. Billy said, "You better fuckin' find it fast. I order you! All I got is this suit I traveled in, and how'm I supposed to shave, brush my teeth, change socks, underpants, and sleep without pajamas?" The government would take care of this, but the messenger was forced to hear that the shirts were made at Sulka's and the suits by the Fifth Avenue tailor who served Winchell, or Jack Dempsey, or top executives at RCA. The designer must have chosen a model from the bird family. The cut of Billy's jacket suggested the elegance of thrushes or robins, dazzling fast walkers, fat in the breast and folded wings upcurved. There the analogy stopped. The rest was complex vanity, peevish haughtiness, cold outrage—a proud-peewee performance, of which the premises were that he was a con-

42

siderable figure, a Broadway personage requiring special consideration, and that he himself owed it to his high show-biz standing to stamp and scream and demand and threaten. Yet all the while, if you looked close at the pink, histrionic, Oriental little face, you saw a small but distinct private sector. It contained quite different data. Billy looked as if he, the *personal* Billy, had other concerns, arising from secret inner reckonings. He had come up from the gutter. That was okay, though, in America the land of opportunity. If he had some gutter in him still, he didn't have to hide it much. In the U.S.A. you could come from nowhere and still stand tall, especially if you had the cash. If you pushed Billy he'd retaliate, and if you can retaliate you've got your self-respect. He could even be a cheapie, it wasn't worth the trouble of covering up. He didn't give a shit who thought what. On the other hand, if he wanted a memorial in Jerusalem, a cultural beauty spot, *that* noble gift was a Billy Rose concept, and don't you forget it. Such components made Billy worth looking at. He combed his hair back like George Raft, or that earlier dude sweetheart Rudolph Valentino. (In the Valentino days, Billy had been a tunesmith in Tin Pan Alley— had composed a little, stolen a little, promoted a whole lot; he still held valuable copyrights.) His look was simultaneously weak and strong. He could claim nothing classic that a well-bred Wasp might claim—a man, say, whose grandfather had gone to Groton, whose remoter ancestors had had the right to wear a breastplate and carry a sword. Weapons were a no-no for Jews in those remoter times, as were blooded horses. Or the big wars.

43

But the best you could do in the present age if you were of privileged descent was to dress in drab expensive good taste and bear yourself with what was left of the Brahmin or Knickerbocker style. By now that, too, was tired and hokey. For Billy, however, the tailored wardrobe was indispensable—like having an executive lavatory of your own. He couldn't present himself without his suits, and this was what fed his anger with El Al and also his despair. This, as he threw his weight around, was how I read him. Noguchi, in what I fancied to be a state of Zen calm, also watched silently as Billy went through his nerve-storm display.

In quieter moments, when he was in the lounge drinking fruit juice and reading messages from New York, Billy looked as if he couldn't stop lamenting the long sufferings of the Jews and, in addition, his own defeats at the hands of fellow Jews. My guess was that his defeats by lady Jews were the most deeply wounding of all. He could win against men. Women, if I was correctly informed, were too much for him.

If he had been an old-time Eastern European Jew, he would have despised such sex defeats. His main connection being with his God, he would have granted no such power to a woman. The sexual misery you read in Billy's looks was an American torment—straight American. Broadway Billy was, moreover, in the pleasure business. Everything, on his New York premises, was resolved in play, in jokes, games, laughs, put-ons, cock teases. And his business efforts were crowned with money. Uneasy lies the head that has no money crown to wear. Billy didn't have to worry about *that*.

Combine these themes, and you can understand Billy's residual wistfulness, his resignation to forces he couldn't control. What he could control he controlled with great effectiveness. But there was so much that counted—how it counted! And how well he knew that he could do nothing about it.

The Fonsteins returned from Galilee sooner than expected. "Gorgeous, but more for the Christians," Sorella said to me. "For instance, the Mount of Beatitudes." She also said, "There wasn't a rowboat big enough for me to sit in. As for swimming, Harry went in, but I didn't bring a bathing suit."

Her comment on Billy's lost luggage was: "It must have embarrassed the hell out of the government. He came to build them a major tourist attraction. If he had kept on hollering, I could see Ben-Gurion himself sitting down at the sewing machine to make him a suit."

The missing bags by then had been recovered—fine-looking articles, like slim leather trunks, brass-bound, and monogrammed. Not from Tiffany, but from the Italian manufacturer who would have supplied Tiffany if Tiffany had sold luggage (obtained through contacts, like the candy and cashmeres of Wolfe the ghostwriter: why should you pay full retail price just because you're a multimillionaire?). Billy gave a press interview and complimented Israel on being part of the modern world. The peevish shadow left his face, and he and Noguchi went out every day to confer on the site of the sculpture garden. The atmosphere at the King David became friendlier. Billy stopped hassling the desk clerks, and the clerks for their part stopped lousing him up. Billy on arrival had made the mistake of asking one of them how much to tip the porter who carried his briefcase to his suite. He said he was not yet at home with the Israeli currency. The clerk had flared up. It made him indignant that a man of such wealth should be miserly with nickels and dimes, and he let him have it. Billy saw to it that the clerk was disciplined by the management. When he heard of this, Fonstein said that in Rome a receptionist in a class hotel would never in the world have made a scene with one of the guests.

"Jewish assumptions," he said. "Not clerks and guests, but one Jew letting another Jew have it—plain talk."

I had expected Harry Fonstein to react strongly to Billy's presence—a guest in the same hotel at prices only the affluent could afford. Fonstein, whom Billy had saved from death, was no more than an undistinguished Jewish American, two tables away in the restaurant. And Fonstein was strong-willed. Under no circumstances would he have approached Billy to introduce himself or to confront him: "I am the man your organization smuggled out of Rome. You brought me to Ellis Island and washed your hands of me, never gave a damn about the future of this refugee. Cut me at Sardi's." No, no, not Harry Fonstein. He understood that there is such a thing as making too much of the destiny of an individual. Besides, it's not really in us nowadays to extend ourselves, to become involved in the fortunes of anyone who happens to approach us.

"Mr. Rose, I am the person you wouldn't see—couldn't fit into your schedule." A look of scalding

46

irony on Fonstein's retributive face. "Now the two of us, in God's eye of terrible judgment, are standing here in this holy city . . ."

Impossible words, an impossible scenario. Nobody says such things, nor would anyone seriously listen if they were said.

No, Fonstein contented himself with observation. You saw a curious light in his eyes when Billy passed, talking to Noguchi. I can't recall a moment when Noguchi replied. Not once did Fonstein discuss with me Billy's presence in the hotel. Again I was impressed with the importance of keeping your mouth shut, the kind of fertility it can induce, the hidden advantages of a buttoned lip.

I did ask Sorella how Fonstein felt at finding Billy here after their trip north.

"A complete surprise."

"Not to you, it wasn't."

"You figured that out, did you?"

"Well, it took no special shrewdness," I said. "I now feel what Dr. Watson must have felt when Sherlock Holmes complimented him on a deduction Holmes had made as soon as the case was outlined to him. Does your husband know about Mrs. Hamet's file?"

"I told him, but I haven't mentioned that I brought the notebook to Jerusalem. Harry is a sound sleeper, whereas I am an insomniac, so I've been up half the night reading the old woman's record, which damns the guy in the suite upstairs. If I didn't have insomnia, this would keep me awake."

"All about his deals, his vices? Damaging stuff?"

47

Sorella first shrugged and then nodded. I believe that she herself was perplexed, couldn't quite make up her mind about it.

"If he were thinking of running for President, he wouldn't like this information made public."

"Sure. But he isn't running. He's not a candidate. He's Broadway Billy, not the principal of a girls' school or pastor of the Riverside Church."

"That's the truth. Still, he is a public person."

I didn't pursue the subject. Certainly Billy was an oddity. On the physical side (and in her character too), Sorella also was genuinely odd. She was so much bigger than the bride I had first met in Lakewood that I couldn't keep from speculating on her expansion. She made you look twice at a doorway. When she came to it, she filled the space like a freighter in a canal lock. In its own right, consciousness—and here I refer to my own conscious mind—was yet another oddity. But the strangeness of souls is certainly no news in this day and age.

Fonstein loved her, that was a clear fact. He respected his wife, and I did too. I wasn't poking fun at either of them when I wondered at her size. I never lost sight of Fonstein's history, or of what it meant to be the survivor of such a destruction. Maybe Sorella was trying to incorporate in fatty tissue some portion of what he had lost—members of his family. There's no telling what she might have been up to. All I can say is that it (whatever it was at bottom) was accomplished with some class or style. Exquisite singers can make you forget what hillocks of suet their backsides are. Besides, Sorella did dead sober what delirious sopranos put over on us in a state of false Wagnerian intoxication.

Her approach to Billy, however, was anything but sober, and I doubt that any sober move would have had an effect on Billy. What she did was to send him several pages, three or four items copied from the journal of that poor consumptive the late Mrs. Hamet. Sorella made sure that the clerk put it in Billy's box, for the material was explosive, and in the wrong hands it might have been deadly.

When this was a *fait accompli,* she told me about it. Too late now to advise her not to do it. "I invited him to have a drink," she said to me.

"Not the three of you . . . ?"

"No. Harry hasn't forgotten the bouncer scene at Sardi's—you may remember—when Billy turned his face to the back of the booth. He'd never again force himself on Billy or any celebrity."

"Billy might still ignore you."

"Well, it's in the nature of an experiment, let's say."

I put aside for once the look of social acceptance so many of us have mastered perfectly and let her see what I thought of her "experiment." She might talk "Science" to her adolescent son, the future physicist. I was not a child you could easily fake out with a prestigious buzzword. Experiment? She was an ingenious and powerful woman who devised intricate, glittering, bristling, needling schemes. What she had in mind was confrontation, a hand-to-hand struggle. The laboratory word was a put-on. "Boldness," "Statecraft," "Passion," "Justice," were the real terms. Still, she may not herself have been clearly aware of this. And then, I later thought, the antagonist *was* Broadway Billy Rose. And she didn't expect him to meet her on the ground she had chosen, did she? What did he care for her big abstractions? He was completely free to say, "I don't know what the fuck you're talking about, and I couldn't care less, lady."

Most interesting—at least to an American mind.

I went about my Mnemosyne business in Jerusalem at a seminar table, unfolding my methods to the Israelis. In the end, Mnemosyne didn't take root in Tel Aviv. (It did thrive in Taiwan and Tokyo.)

On the terrace next day, Sorella, looking pleased and pleasant over her tea, said, "We're going to meet. But he wants me to come to his suite at five o'clock."

"Doesn't want to be seen in public, discussing this . . . ?"

"Exactly."

So she did have real clout, after all. I was sorry now that I hadn't taken the opportunity to read Mrs. Hamet's record. (So much zeal, malice, fury, and tenderness I missed out on.) And I didn't even feel free to ask why Sorella thought Billy had agreed to talk to her. I was sure he wouldn't want to discuss moral theory upstairs. There weren't going to be any revelations, confessions, speculations. People like Billy didn't worry about their deeds, weren't in the habit of accounting to themselves. Very few of us, for that matter, bother about accountability or keep spread sheets of conscience.

What follows is based on Sorella's report and supplemented by my observations. I don't have to say, "If memory serves." In my case it serves, all right. Besides, I made tiny notes, while she was speaking, on the back pages of my appointment book (the yearly gift to depositors in my Philadelphia bank).

Billy's behavior throughout was austere-to-hostile. Mainly he was displeased. His conversation from the first was negative. The King David suite wasn't up to his standards. You had to rough it here in Jerusalem, he said. But the state was young. They'd catch up by and by. These comments were made when he opened the door. He didn't invite Sorella to sit, but at her weight, on her small feet, she wasn't going to be kept standing, and she settled her body in a striped chair, justifying herself by the human sound she made when she seated herself—exhaling as the cushions exhaled.

This was her first opportunity to look Billy over, and she had a few unforeseeable impressions: so this was Billy from the world of the stars. He was very well dressed, in the clothes he had made such a fuss about. At moments you had the feeling that his sleeves were stuffed with the paper tissue used by high-grade cleaners. I had mentioned that there was something birdlike about the cut of his coat, and she agreed with me, but where I saw a robin or a thrush, plump under the shirt, she said (through having installed a bird feeder in New Jersey) that he was more like a grosbeak; he even had some of the color. One eye was set a little closer to the nose than the other, giving a touch of Jewish pathos to his look. Actually, she said, he was a little like Mrs. Hamet, with the one sad eye in her consumptive the-

51

atrical death-white face. And though his hair was groomed, it wasn't absolutely in place. There was a grosbeak disorder about it.

"At first he thought I was here to put the arm on him," she said.

"Money?"

"Sure—probably money."

I kept her going, with nods and half words, as she described this meeting. Of course: blackmail. A man as deep as Billy could call on years of savvy; he had endless experience in handling the people who came to get something out of him—anglers, con artists, crazies.

Billy said, "I glanced over the pages. How much of it is there, and how upset am I supposed to be about it?"

"Deborah Hamet gave me a stack of material before she died."

"Dead, is she?"

"You know she is."

"I don't know anything," said Billy, meaning that this was information from a sector he cared nothing about.

"Yes, but you do," Sorella insisted. "That woman was mad for you."

"That didn't have to be my business, her emotional makeup. She was part of my office force and got her pay. Flowers were sent to White Plains when she got sick. If I had an idea how she was spying, I wouldn't have been so considerate—the dirt that wild old bag was piling up against me."

Sorella told me, and I entirely believed her, that she had come not to threaten but to discuss, to explore, to sound out. She refused to be drawn into a dispute. She could rely on her bulk to give an impression of the fullest calm. Billy had a quantitative cast of mind— businessmen do—and there was lots of woman here. He couldn't deal even with the slenderest of girls. The least of them had the power to put the sexual whammy (Indian sign) on him. Sorella herself saw this. "If he could change my gender, then he could fight me." This was a hint at the masculinity possibly implicit in her huge size. But she had tidy wrists, small feet, a feminine, lyrical voice. She was wearing perfume. She set her lady self before him, massively. . . . What a formidable, clever wife Fonstein had. The protection he lacked when he was in flight from Hitler he had found on our side of the Atlantic.

"Mr. Rose, you haven't called me by name," she said to him. "You read my letter, didn't you? I'm Mrs. Fonstein. Does that ring a bell?"

"And why should it . . . ?" he said, refusing recognition.

"I married Fonstein."

"And my neck size is fourteen. So what?"

"The man you saved in Rome—one of them. He wrote so many letters. I can't believe you don't remember."

"Remember, forget—what's the difference to me?"

"You sent Deborah Hamet to Ellis Island to talk to him."

"Lady, this is one of a trillion incidents in a life like mine. Why should I recollect it?"

Why, yes, I see his point. These details were like the scales of innumerable shoals of fish—the mackerel-

crowded seas: like the particles of those light-annihi-
lating masses, the dense matter of black holes.

"I sent Deborah to Ellis Island—so, okay. . . ."

"With instructions for my husband never to approach
you."

"It's a blank to me. But so what?"

"No personal concern for a man you rescued?"

"I did all I could," said Billy. "And for that point of
time, that's more than most can say. Go holler at Stephen Wise. Raise hell with Sam Rosenman. Guys were
sitting on their hands. They would call on Roosevelt
and Cordell Hull, who didn't care a damn for Jews, and
they were so proud and happy to be close enough to
the White House, even getting the runaround was such
a delicious privilege. FDR snowed those famous rabbis
when they visited him. He blinded them with his foot-
work, that genius cripple. Churchill also was in on this
with him. The goddam white paper. So? There were
refugees by the hundred thousands to ship to Palestine.
Or there wouldn't have been a state here today. That's
why I gave up the single-party rescue operation and
started to raise money to get through the British block-
ade in those rusty Greek tramp ships. . . . Now what do
you want from me—that I didn't receive your husband!
What's the matter? I see you did all right. Now you have
to have special recognition?"

The level, as Sorella was to say to me, being dragged
down, down, downward, the greatness of the events
being beyond anybody's personal scope . . . At times
she would make such remarks.

"Now," Billy asked her, "what do you want with this

54

lousy scandal stuff collected by that cracked old bitch? To embarrass me in Jerusalem, when I came to start this major project?"

Sorella said that she raised both her hands to slow him down. She told him she had come to have a sensible discussion. Nothing threatening had been hinted. . . .

"No! Except that Hamet woman was collecting poison in bottles, and you have the whole collection. Try and place this material in the papers—you'd have to be crazy in the head. If you did try, the stuff would come flying back on you faster than shit through a tin whistle. Look at these charges—that I bribed Robert Moses' people to put across my patriotic Aquacade at the Fair. Or I hired an arsonist to torch a storefront for revenge. Or I sabotaged Baby Snooks because I was jealous of Fanny's big success, and I even tried to poison her. Listen, we still have libel laws. That Hamet was one sick lady. And you—you should stop and think. If not for me, where would you be, a woman like you . . . ?" The meaning was, a woman deformed by obesity.

"Did he say *that*?" I interrupted. But what excited me was not what *he* said. Sorella stopped me in my tracks. I never knew a woman to be so candid about herself. What a demonstration this was of pure objectivity and self-realism. What it signified was that in a time when disguise and deception are practiced so extensively as to numb the powers of awareness, only a major force of personality could produce such admissions. "I *am* built like a Mack truck. My flesh *is* boundless. An Everest of lipoids," she told me. Together with this came, unspoken, an auxiliary admission: she confessed that she was guilty of self-indulgence. This deformity, my outrageous size, an imposition on Fonstein, the brave man who loves me. Who else would want me? All this was fully implicit in the plain, unforced style of her comment. Greatness is the word for such candor, for such an admission, made so naturally. In this world of liars and cowards, there *are* people like Sorella. One waits for them in the blind faith that they *do* exist.

"He was reminding me that he had saved Harry. For me."

Translation: The SS would have liquidated him pretty quick. So except for the magic intervention of this little Lower East Side rat, the starved child who had survived on pastrami trimmings and pushcart apples . . .

Sorella went on. "I explained to Billy: it took Deborah's journal to put me through to him. He had turned his back on us. His answer was, 'I don't need entanglements—what I did, I did. I have to keep down the number of relationships and contacts. What I did for you, take it and welcome, but spare me the relationship and all the rest of it.' "

"I can understand that," I said.

I can't tell you how much I relished Sorella's account of this meeting with Billy. These extraordinary revelations, and also the comments on them that were made. In what he said there was an echo of George Washington's Farewell Address. Avoid entanglements. Billy had to reserve himself for his deals, devote himself body and soul to his superpublicized bad marriages; together with the squalid, rich residences he furnished; plus his gossip columns, his chorus lines, and the awful pursuit of provocative, teasing chicks whom he couldn't do a thing with when they stopped and stripped and waited for him. He had to be free to work his curse out fully. And now he had arrived in Jerusalem to put a top dressing of Jewish grandeur on his chicken-scratch career, on this poor punished N.Y. soil of his. (I am thinking of the tiny prison enclosures—a few black palings— narrow slices of ground preserved at the heart of Manhattan for leaves and grass.) Here Noguchi would create for him a Rose Garden of Sculpture, an art corner within a few kilometers of the stunned desert sloping toward the Dead Sea.

"Tell me, Sorella, what were you after? The objective."

"Billy to meet with Fonstein."

"But Fonstein gave up on him long ago. They must pass each other at the King David every other day. What would be simpler than to stop and say, 'You're Rose? I'm Harry Fonstein. You led me out of Egypt *b'yad hazzakah.*"

"What is that?"

"With a mighty hand. So the Lord God described the rescue of Israel—part of my boyhood basic training. But Fonstein has backed away from this. While you . . ."

"I made up my mind that Billy was going to do right by him."

Yes, sure, of course; Roger; I read you. Something is due from every man to every man. But Billy hadn't

57

heard and didn't want to hear about these generalities.

"If you lived with Fonstein's feelings as I have lived with them," said Sorella, "you'd agree he should get a chance to complete them. To finish out."

In a spirit of high-level discussion, I said to her, "Well, it's a nice idea, only nobody expects to complete their feelings anymore. They have to give up on closure. It's just not available."

"For some it is."

So I was obliged to think again. Sure—what about the history of Sorella's own feelings? She had been an unwanted Newark French teacher until her Havana uncle had a lucky hunch about Fonstein. They were married, and thanks to him, she obtained her closure, she became the tiger wife, the tiger mother, grew into a biological monument and a victorious personality . . . a figure!

But Billy's reply was: "So what's it got to do with me?"

"Spend fifteen minutes alone with my husband," she said to him.

Billy refused her. "It's not the kind of thing I do."

"A handshake, and he'll say thanks."

"First of all, I warned you already about libel, and as for the rest, what do you think you're holding over me anyway? I wouldn't do this. You haven't convinced me that I must. I don't like things from the past being laid on me. This happened one time, years ago. What's it got to do with now—1959? If your husband has a nice story, that's his good luck. Let him tell it to people who go for stories. I don't care for them. I don't care for my

58

own story. If I had to listen to it, I'd break out in a cold sweat. And I wouldn't go around and shake everybody's hand unless I was running for mayor. That's why I never would run. I shake when I close a deal. Otherwise, my hands stay in my pockets.''

Sorella said, "Since Deborah Hamet had given me the goods on him and the worst could be assumed, he stood up to me on the worst basis, with all the bruises on his reputation, under every curse—grungy, weak, cheap, perverted. He made me take him for what he was—a kinky little kike finagler whose life history was one disgrace after another. Take this man: He never flew a single mission, never hunted big game, never played football or went down in the Pacific. Never even tried suicide. And this reject was a celeb! . . . You know, Deborah had a hundred ways to say celeb. Mostly she cut him down, but a celeb is still a celeb—you can't take that away. When American Jews decided to make a statement about the War Against the Jews, they had to fill Madison Square Garden with big-name celebs singing Hebrew and 'America the Beautiful.' Hollywood stars blowing the *shofar*. The man to produce this spectacular and arrange the press coverage was Billy. They turned to him, and he took total charge. . . . How many people does the Garden hold? Well, it was full, and everybody was in mourning. I suppose the whole place was in tears. The *Times* covered it, which is the paper of record, so the record shows that the American Jewish way was to assemble twenty-five thousand people, Hollywood style, and weep publicly for what had happened.''

Continuing her report on her interview with Billy, Sorella said that he adopted what negotiators call a bargaining posture. He behaved as though he had reason to be proud of his record, of the deals he had made, and I suppose that he was standing his ground behind this front of pride. Sorella hadn't yet formulated her threat. Beside her on a chair that decorators would have called a love seat there lay (and he saw) a large manila envelope. It contained Deborah's papers—what else would she have brought to his suite? To make a grab for this envelope was out of the question. "I outreached him and outweighed him," said Sorella. "I could scratch him as well, and also shriek. And the very thought of a scene, a scandal, would have made him sick. Actually, the man was looking sick. His calculation in Jerusalem was to make a major gesture, to enter Jewish history, attaining a level far beyond show biz. He had seen only a sample of the Hamet/Horsecollar file. But imagine what the newspapers, the world tabloid press, could do with this material.

"So he was waiting to hear my proposition," said Sorella.

I said, "I'm trying to figure out just what you had in mind."

"Concluding a chapter in Harry's life. It should be concluded," said Sorella. "It was a part of the destruction of the Jews. On our side of the Atlantic, where we weren't threatened, we have a special duty to come to terms with it. . . ."

"Come to terms? Who, Billy Rose?"

"Well, he involved himself in it actively."

I recall that I shook my head and said, "You were asking too much. You couldn't have gotten very far with him."

"Well, he did say that Fonstein suffered much less than others. He wasn't in Auschwitz. He got a major break. He wasn't tattooed with a number. They didn't put him to work cremating the people that were gassed. I said to Billy that the Italian police must have been under orders to hand Jews over to the SS and that so many were shot in Rome, in the Ardeatine Caves."

"What did he say to this?"

"He said, 'Look, lady, why do I have to think about all of that? I'm not the kind of guy who's expected to. This is too much for me.' I said, 'I'm not asking you to make an enormous mental effort, only to sit down with my husband for fifteen minutes.' 'Suppose I do,' he said. 'What's your offer?' 'I'll hand over Deborah's whole file. I've got it right here.' 'And if I don't play ball?' 'Then I'll turn it over to some other party, or parties.' Then he burst out, 'You think you've got me by the knackers, don't you? You're taking an unfair terrible advantage of me. I don't want to talk dirty to a respectable person, but I call this kicking the shit out of a man. Right now I'm in an extrasensitive position, considering what's my purpose in Jerusalem. I want to contribute a memorial. Maybe it would be better not to leave any reminder of my life and I should be forgotten altogether. So at this moment you come along to take revenge from the grave for a jealous woman. I can imagine the record this crazy put together, about deals I made—I know she got the business part all wrong, and the bribery and arson would never stick. So that leaves things like the private clinical junk collected from show girls who bad-mouthed me. But let me say one thing, Missus: Even a geek has his human rights. Last of all, I haven't got all that many secrets left. It's all been told.' 'Almost all,' I said."

I observed, "You sure did bear down hard on him."

"Yes, I did," she admitted. "But he fought back. The libel suits he threatened were only bluff, and I told him so. I pointed out how little I was asking. Not even a note to Harry, just a telephone message would be enough, and then fifteen minutes of conversation. Mulling it over, with his eyes cast down and his little hands passive on the back of a sofa—he was on his feet, he wouldn't sit down, that would seem like a concession— he refused me again. Once and for all he said he wouldn't meet with Harry. 'I already did for him all I'm able to do.' 'Then you leave me no alternative,' I said."

On the striped chair in Billy's suite, Sorella opened her purse to look for a handkerchief. She touched herself on the temples and on the folds of her arms, at the elbow joint. The white handkerchief looked no bigger than a cabbage moth. She dried herself under the chin.

"He must have shouted at you," I said.

"He began to yell at me. It was what I anticipated, a screaming fit. He said no matter what you did, there was always somebody waiting with a switchblade to cut you, or acid to throw in your face, or claws to rip the clothes off you and leave you naked. That fucking old Hamet broad, whom he kept out of charity—as if her eyes weren't kooky enough, she put on those giant crooked round goggles. She hunted up those girls who swore he had the sexual development of a ten-year-old boy. It didn't matter for shit, because he was humiliated all his life long and you couldn't do more than was done already. There was relief in having no more to cover up. He didn't care what Hamet had written down, that bitch-eye mummy, spitting blood and saving the last glob for the man she hated most. As for me, I was a heap of fat filth!"

"You don't have to repeat it all, Sorella."

"Then I won't. But I did lose my temper. My dignity fell apart."

"Do you mean that you wanted to hit him?"

"I threw the document at him. I said, 'I don't *want* my husband to talk to the likes of you. You're not fit . . .' I aimed Deborah's packet at him. But I'm not much good at throwing, and it went through the open window."

"What a moment! What did Billy do then?"

"All the rage was wiped out instantly. He picked up the phone and got the desk. He said, 'A very important document was dropped from my window. I want it brought up right now. You understand? Immediately. This minute.' I went to the door. I don't suppose I wanted to make a gesture, but I am a Newark girl at bottom. I said, 'You're the filth. I want no part of you.' And I made the Italian gesture people used to make in a street fight, the edge of the palm on the middle of my arm."

Inconspicuously, and laughing as she did it, she made a small fist and drew the edge of her other hand across her biceps.

"A very American conclusion."

"Oh," she said, "from start to finish it was a one-hundred-percent American event, of our own generation. It'll be different for our children. A kid like our Gilbert, at his mathematics summer camp? Let him for the rest of his life do nothing but mathematics. Nothing could be more different from either East Side tenements or the back streets of Newark."

All this had happened toward the end of the Fonsteins' visit, and I'm sorry now that I didn't cancel a few Jerusalem appointments for their sake—give them dinner at Dagim Benny, a good fish restaurant. It would have been easy enough for me to clear the decks. What, to spend more time in Jerusalem with a couple from New Jersey named Fonstein? Yes is the answer. Today it's a matter of regret. The more I think of Sorella, the more charm she has for me.

I remember saying to her, "I'm sorry you didn't hit Billy with that packet."

My thought, then and later, was that she was too much hampered by fat under the arms to make an accurate throw.

She said, "As soon as the envelope left my hands I realized that I longed to get rid of it, and of everything connected with it. Poor Deborah—Mrs. Horsecollar, as you like to call her. I see that I was wrong to identify myself with her cause, her tragic life. It makes you think about the high and the low in people. Love is supposed to be high, but imagine falling for a creature like Billy.

I didn't want a single thing that man could give Harry and me. Deborah recruited me, so I would continue her campaign against him, keep the heat on from the grave. He was right about that."

This was our very last conversation. Beside the King David driveway, she and I were waiting for Fonstein to come down. The luggage had been stowed in the Mercedes—at that time, every other cab in Jerusalem was a Mercedes-Benz. Sorella said to me, "How do you see the whole Billy business?"

In those days I still had the Villager's weakness for theorizing—the profundity game so popular with middle-class boys and girls in their bohemian salad days. Ring anybody's bell, and he'd open the window and empty a basin full of thoughts on your head.

"Billy views everything as show biz," I said. "Nothing is real that isn't a show. And he wouldn't perform in your show because he's a producer, and producers don't perform."

To Sorella, this was not a significant statement, so I tried harder. "Maybe the most interesting thing about Billy is that he wouldn't meet with Harry," I said. "He wasn't able to be the counterexample in a case like Harry's. Couldn't begin to measure up."

Sorella said, "That may be a little more like it. But if you want my basic view, here it is: The Jews could survive everything that Europe threw at them. I mean the lucky remnant. But now comes the next test—America. Can they hold their ground, or will the U.S.A. be too much for them?"

This was our final meeting. I never saw Harry and Sorella again. In the sixties, Harry telephoned once to discuss Cal Tech with me. Sorella didn't want Gilbert to study so far from home. An only child, and all of that. Harry was full of the boy's perfect test scores. My heart doesn't warm to the parents of prodigies. I react badly. They're riding for a fall. I don't like parental boasting. So I was unable to be cordial toward Fonstein. My time just then was unusually valuable. Horribly valuable, as I now judge it. Not one of the attractive periods in the development (gestation) of a success.

I can't say that communication with the Fonsteins ceased. Except in Jerusalem, we hadn't had any. I expected, for thirty years, to see them again. They were excellent people. I admired Harry. A solid man, Harry, and very brave. As for Sorella, she was a woman with great powers of intelligence, and in these democratic times, whether you are conscious of it or not, you are continually in quest of higher types. I don't have to draw you maps and pictures. Everybody knows what standard products and interchangeable parts signify, understands the operation of the glaciers on the social landscape, planing off the hills, scrubbing away the irregularities. I'm not going to be tedious about this. Sorella was outstanding (or as one of my grandchildren says, "standing out"). So of course I meant to see more of her. But I saw nothing. She was in the warehouse of intentions. I was going to get around to the

Fonsteins—write, telephone, have them for Thanksgiving, for Christmas. Perhaps for Passover. But that's what the Passover phenomenon is now—it never comes to pass.

Maybe the power of memory was to blame. Remembering them so well, did I need actually to *see* them? To keep them in a mental suspension was enough. They were a part of the permanent cast of characters, in absentia permanently. There wasn't a thing for them to do.

The next in this series of events occurred last March, when winter, with a grunt, gave up its grip on Philadelphia and began to go out in trickles of grimy slush. Then it was the turn of spring to thrive on the dirt of the city. The season at least produced crocuses, snowdrops, and new buds in my millionaire's private back garden. I pushed around my library ladder and brought down the poems of George Herbert, looking for the one that runs ". . . how clean, how pure are Thy returns," or words to that effect; and on my desk, fit for a Wasp of great wealth, the phone started to ring as I was climbing down. The following Jewish conversation began:

"This is Rabbi X [or Y]. My ministry"—what a Protestant term: he must be Reform, or Conservative at best; no Orthodox rabbi would say "ministry"—"is in Jerusalem. I have been approached by a party whose name is Fonstein. . . ."

"Not Harry," I said.

"No. I was calling to ask *you* about locating Harry. The Jerusalem Fonstein says that he is Harry's uncle. This man is Polish by birth, and he is in a mental institution. He is a very difficult eccentric and lives in a world of fantasy. Much of the time he hallucinates. His habits are dirty—filthy, even. He's totally without resources and well known as a beggar and local character who makes prophetic speeches on the sidewalk."

"I get the picture. Like one of our own homeless," I said.

"Precisely," said Rabbi X or Y, in that humane tone of voice one has to put up with.

"Can we come to the point?" I asked.

"Our Jerusalem Fonstein swears he is related to Harry, who is very rich. . . ."

"I've never seen Harry's financial statement."

"But in a position to help."

I went on, "That's just an opinion. At a hazard . . ." One does get pompous. A solitary, occupying a mansion, living up to his surroundings. I changed my tune; I dropped the "hazard" and said, "It's been years since Harry and I were in touch. You can't locate him?"

"I've tried. I'm on a two-week visit. Right now I'm in New York. But L.A. is my destination. Addressing . . ." (He gave an unfamiliar acronym.) Then he went on to say that the Jerusalem Fonstein needed help. Poor man, absolutely bananas, but under all the tatters, physical and mental (I paraphrase), humanly so worthy. Abused out of his head by persecution, loss, death, and brutal history; beside himself, crying out for aid—human and supernatural, no matter in what mixture. There may have been something phony about the rabbi, but the case, the man he was describing, was a familiar type, was real enough.

"And you, too, are a relative?" he said.

"Indirectly. My father's second wife was Harry's aunt."

I never loved Aunt Mildred, nor even esteemed her. But, you understand, she had a place in my memory, and there must have been a good reason for that.

"May I ask you to find him for me and give him my number in L.A.? I'm carrying a list of family names and Harry Fonstein will recognize, will identify him. Or will not, if the man is *not* his uncle. It would be a mitzvah."

Christ, spare me these mitzvahs.

I said, "Okay, Rabbi, I'll trace Harry, for the sake of this pitiable lunatic."

The Jerusalem Fonstein gave me a pretext for getting in touch with the Fonsteins. (Or at least an incentive.) I entered the rabbi's number in my book, under the last address I had for Fonstein. At the moment, there were other needs and duties requiring my attention; besides, I wasn't yet ready to speak to Sorella and Harry. There were preparations to make. This, as it appears under my ballpoint, reminds me of the title of Stanislavski's famous book, *An Actor Prepares*—again, a datum relating to my memory, a resource, a vocation, to which a lifetime of cultivation has been devoted, and which in old age also oppresses me.

For just then (meaning now: "Now, now, very now") I was, I am, having difficulties with it. I had had a failure of memory the other morning, and it had driven me almost mad (not to hold back on an occurrence of such importance). I had had a dental appointment downtown. I drove, because I was already late and couldn't rely on the radio cab to come on time. I parked in a lot blocks away, the best I could do on a busy morning, when closer lots were full. Then, walking back from the dentist's office, I found (under the influence of my walking rhythm, I presume) that I had a tune in my head. The words came to me:

> Way down upon the . . .
> Way down upon the . . .
> . . . upon the ——— River . . .

But what was the river called! A song I'd sung from childhood, upwards of seventy years, part of the foundations of one's mind. A classic song, known to all Americans. Of my generation anyway.

I stopped at the window of a sports shop, specializing, as it happened, in horsemen's boots, shining boots, both men's and women's, plaid saddle blankets, crimson coats, fox-hunting stuff—even brass horns. All objects on display were ultrasignificantly distinct. The colors of the plaid were especially bright and orderly— enviably orderly to a man whose mind was at that instant shattered.

What was that river's name!

I could easily recall the rest of the words:

> There's where my heart is yearning ever,
> That's where the old folks stay.
> All the world is [am?] sad and dreary

Everywhere I roam.
O darkies, how my heart grows weary . . .

And the rest.

All the world *was* dark and dreary. Fucking-A right! A chip, a plug, had gone dead in the mental apparatus. A forerunning omen? Beginning of the end? There are psychic causes of forgetfulness, of course. I've lectured on those myself. Not everyone, needless to say, would take such a lapsus so to heart. A bridge was broken: I could not cross the ——— River. I had an impulse to hammer the window of the riding shop with the handle of my umbrella, and when people ran out, to cry to them, "Oh, God! You must tell me the words. I can't get past 'Way down upon the . . . upon the!'" They would—I saw it—throw that red saddle cloth, a brilliant red, threads of fire, over my shoulders and take me into the shop to wait for the ambulance.

At the parking lot, I wanted to ask the cashier—out of desperation. When she said, "Seven dollars," I would begin singing the tune through the round hole in the glass. But as the woman was black, she might be offended by "O darkies." And could I assume that she, like me, had been brought up on Stephen Foster? There were no grounds for this. For the same reason, I couldn't ask the car jockey either.

But at the wheel of the car, the faulty connection corrected itself, and I began to shout, "Swanee—Swanee—Swanee," punching the steering wheel. Behind the windows of your car, what you do doesn't matter. One of the privileges of liberty car ownership affords.

71

Of course! The Swanee. Or Suwannee (spelling preferred in the South). But this was a crisis in my mental life. I had had a double purpose in looking up George Herbert—not only the appropriateness of the season but as a test of my memory. So, too, my recollection of *Fonstein* v. *Rose* is in part a test of memory, and also a more general investigation of the same, for if you go back to the assertion that memory is life and forgetting death ("mercifully forgetting," the commonest adverb linked by writers with the participle, reflecting the preponderance of the opinion that so much of life *is* despair), I have established at the very least that I am still able to keep up my struggle for existence.

Hoping for victory? Well, what would a victory be?

I took Rabbi X/Y's word for it that the Fonsteins had moved away and were unlocatable. Probably they had, like me, retired. But whereas I am in Philadelphia, hanging in there, as the idiom puts it, they had very likely abandoned that ground of struggle the sullen North and gone to Sarasota or to Palm Springs. They had the money for it. America was good to Harry Fonstein, after all, and delivered on its splendid promises. He had been spared the worst we have here—routine industrial or clerical jobs and bureaucratic employment. As I wished the Fonsteins well, I was pleased for them. My much-appreciated in-absentia friends, so handsomely installed in my consciousness.

Not having heard from me, I assumed, they had given up on me, after three decades. Freud has laid down the principle that the unconscious does not recognize death. But as you see, consciousness is freaky too.

So I went to work digging up forgotten names of relatives from my potato-patch mind—Rosenberg, Rosenthal, Sorkin, Swerdlow, Bleistiff, Fradkin. Jewish surnames are another curious subject, so many of them imposed by German, Polish, or Russian officialdom (expecting bribes from applicants), others the invention of Jewish fantasy. How often the name of the rose was invoked, as in the case of Billy himself. There were few other words for flowers in the pale. *Margaritka,* for one. The daisy. Not a suitable family name for anybody.

Aunt Mildred, my stepmother, had been cared for during her last years by relatives in Elizabeth, the Rosensafts, and my investigations began with them. They weren't cordial or friendly on the phone, because I had seldom visited Mildred toward the last. I think she began to claim that she had brought me up and even put me through college. (The funds came from a Prudential policy paid for by my own mother.) This was a venial offense, which gave me the reasons for being standoffish that I was looking for. I wasn't fond of the Rosensafts either. They had taken my father's watch and chain after he died. But then one can live without these objects of sentimental value. Old Mrs. Rosensaft said she had lost track of the Fonsteins. She thought the Swerdlows in Morristown might know where Harry and Sorella had gone.

Information gave me Swerdlow's number. Dialing, I reached an answering machine. The voice of Mrs. Swerdlow, affecting an accent more suitable to upper-class Morristown than to her native Newark, asked me to leave my name, number, and the date of the call. I hate answering machines, so I hung up. Besides, I avoid giving my unlisted number.

As I went up to my second-floor office that night holding the classic Philadelphia banister, reflecting that I was pretty sick of the unshared grandeur of this mansion, I once more considered Sarasota or the sociable Florida Keys. Elephants and acrobats, circuses in winter quarters, would be more amusing. Moving to Palm Springs was out of the question. And while the Keys had a large homosexual population, I was more at home with gay people, thanks to my years in the Village, than with businessmen in California. In any case, I couldn't bear much more of these thirty-foot ceilings and all the mahogany solitude. This mansion demanded too much from me, and I was definitely conscious of a strain. My point had long ago been made—I could achieve such a dwelling place, possess it in style. Now take it away, I thought, in a paraphrase of the old tune "I'm so tired of roses, take them all away." I decided to discuss the subject again with my son, Henry. His wife didn't like the mansion; her tastes were modern, and she was satirical, too, about the transatlantic rivalry of parvenu American wealth with the titled wealth of Victorian London. She had turned me down dead flat when I tried to give the place to them.

What I was thinking was that if I could find Harry and Sorella, I'd join them in retirement, if they'd accept my company (forgiving the insult of neglect). For me it was natural to wonder whether I had not exaggerated (urged on by a desire for a woman of a deeper nature) Sorella's qualities in my reminiscences, and I gave fur-

74

ther thought to this curious personality. I never had forgotten what she had said about the testing of Jewry by the American experience. Her interview with Billy Rose had itself been such an American thing. Again Billy: Weak? Weak! Vain? Oh, very! And trivial for sure. Creepy Billy. Still, in a childish way, big-minded—spacious; and spacious wasn't just a boast adjective from "America the Beautiful" (the spacious skies) but the dropping of fifteen to twenty actual millions on a rest-and-culture garden in Jerusalem, the core of Jewish history, the navel of the earth. This gesture of oddball magnificence was American. American and Oriental.

And even if I didn't in the end settle near the Fonsteins, I could pay them a visit. I couldn't help asking why I had turned away from such a terrific pair—Sorella, so mysteriously obese; Fonstein with his reddish skin (once stone white), his pomegranate face. I may as well include myself, as a third—a tall old man with a structural curl at the top like a fiddlehead fern or a bishop's crook.

Therefore I started looking for Harry and Sorella not merely because I had promised Rabbi X/Y, nor for the sake of the crazy old man in Jerusalem who was destitute. If it was only money that he needed, I could easily write a check or ask my banker to send him one. The bank charges eight bucks for this convenience, and a phone call would take care of it. But I preferred to attend to things in my own way, from my mansion office, dialing the numbers myself, bypassing the Mnemosyne Institute and its secretaries.

Using old address books, I called all over the place.

(If only cemeteries had switchboards. "Hello, Operator, I'm calling area code 000.") I didn't want to involve the girls at the Institute in any of this, least of all in my investigations. When I reached a number, the conversation was bound to be odd, and a strain on the memory of the Founder. "Why, how are you?" somebody would ask whom I hadn't seen in three decades. "Do you remember my husband, Max? My daughter, Zoe?" Would I know what to say?

Yes, I would. But then again, why should I? How nice oblivion would be in such cases, and I could say, "Max? Zoe? No, I can't say that I do." On the fringes of the family, or in remote, time-dulled social circles, random memories can be an affliction. What you see first, retrospectively, are the psychopaths, the uglies, the cheapies, the stingies, the hypochondriacs, the family bores, humanoids, and tyrants. These have dramatic staying power. Harder to recover are the kind eyes, gentle faces, of the comedians who wanted to entertain you, gratis, divert you from troubles. An important part of my method is that memory chains are constructed thematically. Where themes are lacking there can be little or no recall. So, for instance, Billy, our friend Bellarosa, could not easily place Fonstein because of an unfortunate thinness of purely human themes—as contrasted with business, publicity, or sexual themes. To give a strongly negative example, there are murderers who can't recall their crimes because they have no interest in the existence or nonexistence of their victims. So, students, only pertinent themes assure full recollection.

Some of the old people I reached put me down spiritedly: "If you remember so much about me, how come I haven't seen you since the Korean War! . . ." "No, I can't tell you anything about Salkind's niece Sorella. Salkind came home to New Jersey after Castro took over. He died in an old people's nursing racket setup back in the late sixties."

One man commented, "The pages of calendars crumble away. They're like the dandruff of time. What d'you want from me?"

Calling from a Philadelphia mansion, I was at a disadvantage. A person in my position will discover, in contact with people from Passaic, Elizabeth, or Paterson, how many defenses he has organized against vulgarity or the lower grades of thought. I didn't want to talk about Medicare or social security checks or hearing aids or pacemakers or bypass surgery.

From a few sources I heard criticisms of Sorella. "Salkind was a bachelor, had no children, and that woman should have done something for the old fella."

"He never married?"

"Never," said the bitter lady I had on the line. "But he married *her* off, for his own brother's sake. Anyway, they've all checked out, so what's the diff."

"And you can't tell me where I might find Sorella?"

"I could care less."

"No," I said. "You couldn't care less."

So the matchmaker himself had been a lifelong bachelor. He had disinterestedly found a husband for his brother's daughter, bringing together two disadvantaged people.

Another lady said about Sorella, "She was remote.

77

She looked down on my type of conversation. I think she was a snob. I tried to sign her up once for a group tour in Europe. My temple sisterhood put together a real good charter-flight package. Then Sorella told me that French was her second language, and she didn't need anybody to interpret for her in Paris. I should have told her, 'I knew you when no man would give you a second look and would even take back the first look if he could.' So that's how it was. Sorella was too good for everybody. . . ."

I saw what these ladies meant (this was a trend among my informants). They accused Mrs. Fonstein of being uppish, too grand. Almost all were offended. She preferred the company of Mrs. Hamet, the old actress with the paraffin-white tubercular face. Sorella was too grand for Billy too; hurling Mrs. Hamet's deadly dossier at him was the gesture of a superior person, a person of intelligence and taste. Queenly, imperial, and inevitably isolated. This was the consensus of all the gossips, the elderly people I telephoned from the triple isolation of my Philadelphia residence.

The Fonsteins and I were meant to be company for one another. They weren't going to force themselves on me, however. They assumed that I was above them socially, in upper-class Philadelphia, and that I didn't want their friendship. I don't suppose that my late wife, Deirdre, would have cared for Sorella, with her pince-nez and high manner, the working of her intellect and the problems of her cumulous body—trying to fit itself into a Hepplewhite chair in our dining room. Fonstein would have been comparatively easy for Deirdre to be with. Still, if I was not an assimilationist, I was at least an avoider of uncomfortable mixtures, and in the end I am stuck with these twenty empty rooms.

I can remember driving with my late father through western Pennsylvania. He was struck by the amount of land without a human figure in it. So much space! After long silence, in a traveler's trance resembling the chessboard trance, he said, "Ah, how many Jews might have been settled here! Room enough for everybody."

At times I feel like a socket that remembers its tooth.

As I made call after call, I was picturing my reunion with the Fonsteins. I had them placed mentally in Sarasota, Florida, and imagined the sunny strolls we might take in the winter quarters of Ringling or Hagenbeck, chatting about events long past at the King David Hotel—Billy Rose's lost suitcases, Noguchi's Oriental reserve. In old manila envelopes I found color snapshots from Jerusalem, among them a photograph of Fonstein and Sorella against the background of the Judean desert, the burning stones of Ezekiel, not yet (even today) entirely cooled, those stones of fire among which the cherubim had walked. In that fierce place, two modern persons, the man in a business suit, the woman in floating white, a married couple holding hands—her fat palm in his inventor's fingers. I couldn't help thinking that Sorella didn't have a real biography until Harry entered her life. And he, Harry, whom Hitler had intended to kill, had a biography insofar as Hitler had marked him for murder, insofar as he had fled, was saved by Billy, reached America, invented a better thermostat. And here they were in color, the Judean desert behind them, as husband and wife in a once-upon-a-time Coney Island might have posed against a painted backdrop or sitting on a slice of moon. As tourists in the Holy Land where were they, I wondered, biographically speaking? How memorable had this trip been for them? The question sent me back to myself and, Jewish style, answered itself with yet another question: What was there worth remembering?

When I got to the top of the stairs—this was the night before last—I couldn't bring myself to go to bed just yet. One does grow weary of taking care of this man-sized doll, the elderly retiree, giving him his pills, pulling on his socks, spooning up his cornflakes, shaving his face, seeing to it that he gets his sleep. Instead of opening the bedroom door, I went to my second-floor sitting room.

To save myself from distraction by concentrating every kind of business in a single office, I do bills, bank statements, legal correspondence on the ground floor, and my higher activities I carry upstairs. Deirdre had approved of this. It challenged her to furnish each setting appropriately. One of my diversions is to make the rounds of antiques shops and look at comparable pieces, examining and pricing them, noting what a shrewd buyer Deirdre had been. In doing this, I build a case against remaining in Philadelphia, a town in which a man finds little else to do with himself on a dull afternoon.

Even the telephone in my second-story room is a French instrument with a porcelain mouthpiece—blue and white Quimper. Deirdre had bought it on the Boulevard Haussmann, and Baron Charlus might have romanced his boyfriends with it, speaking low and scheming intricately into this very phone. It would have amused him, if he haunted objects of common use, to watch me dialing the Swerdlows' number again, pursuing my Fonstein inquiries.

On this *art nouveau* article—for those who escape from scientific ignorance (how *do* telephones operate?) with the aid of high-culture toys—I tried Morristown again, and this time Hyman Swerdlow himself answered. As soon as I heard his voice, he appeared before me, and presently his wife also was reborn in my memory and stood beside him. Swerdlow, who was directly related to Fonstein, had been an investment counselor. Trained on Wall Street, he settled in stylish New Jersey. He was a respectable, smooth person, very quiet in manner, "understated," to borrow a term from the interior decorators. His look was both saturnine and guilt-free. He probably didn't like what he had made of his life, but there was no way to revise that now. He settled for good manners—he was very polite, he wore Brooks Brothers grays and tans. His tone was casual. One could assimilate now *without* converting. You didn't have to choose between Jehovah and Jesus. I had known old Swerdlow. His son had inherited an ancient Jewish face from him, dark and craggy. Hyman had discovered a way to drain the Jewish charge from it. What replaced it was a look of perfect dependability. He was well-spoken. He could be trusted with your pension funds. He wouldn't dream of making a chancy investment. His children were a biochemist and a molecular biologist, respectively. His wife could now devote herself to her watercolor box.

I believe the Swerdlows were very intelligent. They may even have been deeply intelligent. What had happened to them couldn't have been helped.

"I can't tell you anything about Fonstein," Swerdlow said. "I've somehow lost track. . . ."

I realized that, like the Fonsteins, Swerdlow and his wife had isolated themselves. No deliberate choice was made. You went your own way, and you found yourself in Greater New York but beyond the bedroom communities, decently situated. Your history, too, became one of your options. Whether or not having a history was a "consideration" was entirely up to you.

Cool Swerdlow, who of course remembered me (I was rich, I might have become an important client; there was, however, no reproach detectable in his tone), now was asking what I wanted with Harry Fonstein. I said that a mad old man in Jerusalem needed Fonstein's help. Swerdlow dropped his inquiry then and there. "We never did develop a relationship," he said. "Harry was very decent. His wife, however, was somewhat overpowering."

Decoded, this meant that Edna Swerdlow had not taken to Sorella. One learns soon enough to fill in the simple statements to which men like Swerdlow limit themselves. They avoid putting themselves out and they shun (perhaps even hate) psychological elaboration.

"When did you last see the Fonsteins?"

"During the Lakewood period," said tactful Swerdlow—he avoided touching upon my father's death, possibly a painful subject. "I think it was when Sorella talked so much about Billy Rose."

"They were involved with him. *He* refused to be drawn in. . . . So you heard them talking about it?"

"Even sensible people lose their heads over celebrities. What claim did Harry have on Billy Rose, and why *should* Billy have done more than he did? A man like Rose has to ration the number of people he can take on."

"Like a sign in an elevator—'Maximum load twenty-eight hundred pounds'?"

"If you like."

"When I think of the Fonstein-Billy thing," I said, "I'm liable to see European Jewry also. What was all *that* about? To me, the operational term is Justice. Once and for all it was seen that this expectation, or reliance, had no foundation. You had to forget about justice . . . whether, taken seriously for so long, it could be taken seriously still."

Swerdlow could not allow me to go on. This was not his kind of conversation. "Put it any way you like—how does it apply to Billy? What was *he* supposed to do about it?"

Well, I didn't expect Billy to take this, or anything else, upon himself. From Hyman Swerdlow I felt that speaking of Justice was not only out of place but off the wall. And if the Baron Charlus had been listening, haunting his telephone with the Quimper mouthpiece, he would have turned from this conversation with contempt. I didn't greatly blame myself, and I certainly did not feel like a fool. At worst it had been inappropriate to call Swerdlow for information and then, without preparation, swerve wildly into such a subject, trying to carry him with me. These were matters I thought about privately, the subjective preoccupations of a person who lived alone in a great Philadelphia house in which he felt out of place, and who had lost sight of the difference between brooding and permissible conversation. I had no business out of the blue to talk to Swerdlow about Justice or Honor or the Platonic Ideas or the expectations of the Jews. Anyway, his tone now made it clear that he wanted to get rid of me, so I said, "This Rabbi X/Y from Jerusalem, who speaks better than fair English, got me to promise that I would locate Fonstein. He said he hadn't been able to find him."

"Are you sure that Fonstein isn't listed in the directory?"

No, I wasn't sure, was I? I hadn't looked. That was just like me, wasn't it? "I assumed the rabbi *had* looked," I said. "I feel chastened. I shouldn't have taken the man's word for it. *He* should have looked. I took it for granted. You're probably right."

"If I can be of further use . . . ?"

By pointing out how he would have gone about finding Fonstein, Swerdlow showed me how lopsided I was. Sure it was stupid of me not to look in the phone directory. Smart, smart, but a dope, as the old people used to say. For the Fonsteins *were* listed. Information gave me their number. There they were, as accessible as millions of others, in small print, row on row on row, the endless listings.

I dialed the Fonsteins, braced for a conversation—my opening words prepared, my excuses for neglecting them made with warmth, just such warmth as I actually felt. Should they be inclined to blame me—well, I was to blame.

But they were out, or had unplugged their line. Elderly people, they probably turned in early. After a dozen rings, I gave up and went to bed myself. And when I got into bed—without too much fear of being alone in this huge place, not that there aren't plenty of murdering housebreakers in the city—I picked up a book, preparing to settle in for a long read.

Deirdre's bedside books had now become mine. I was curious to know how she had read herself to sleep. What had been on her mind became important to me. In her last years she had turned to such books as *Koré Kosmu*, the *Hermetica* published by Oxford, and also selections from the Zohar. Like the heroine of Poe's story "Morella." Odd that Deirdre had said so little about it. She was not a secretive lady, but like many others she kept her own counsel in matters of thought and religion. I loved to see her absorbed in a book, mummied up on her side of the antique bed, perfectly still under the covers. A pair of lamps on each side were like bronze thornbushes. I was always after Deirdre to get sensible reading lights. Nothing could persuade her—she was obstinate when her taste was challenged—and three years after she passed away I was still shopping: Those sculpture brambles never will be replaced.

Some men fall asleep on the sofa after dinner. This often results in insomnia, and as I hate to be up in the night, my routine is to read in bed until midnight, concentrating on passages marked by Deirdre and on her notes at the back of the book. It has become one of my sentimental rituals.

But on this night I passed out after a few sentences, and presently I began to dream.

There is great variety in my dreams. My nights are often busy. I have anxious dreams, amusing dreams, desire dreams, symbolic dreams. There are, however, dreams that are all business and go straight to the point. I suppose we have the dreams we deserve, and they may even be prepared in secret.

Without preliminaries, I found myself in a hole. Night, a dark plain, a pit, and from the start I was already trying to climb out. In fact, I had been working at it for some time. This was a dug hole, not a grave but a trap prepared for me by somebody who knew me well enough to anticipate that I would fall in. I could see over the edge, but I couldn't crawl out because my legs were tangled and caught in ropes or roots. I was clawing at the dirt for something I could grip. I had to rely on my arms. If I could hoist myself onto the edge, I might free the lower body. Only, I was already exhausted, winded, and if I did manage to pull myself out, I'd be too beat to fight. My struggles were watched by the person who had planned this for me. I could see his boots. Down the way, in a similar ditch, another man was also wearing himself out. He wasn't going to make it either. Despair was not principally what I felt, nor fear of death. What made the dream terrible was my complete conviction of error, my miscalculation of strength, and the recognition that my forces were drained to the bottom. The whole structure was knocked flat. There wasn't a muscle in me that I hadn't called on, and for the first time I was aware of them all, down to the tiniest, and the best they could do was not enough. I couldn't call on myself, couldn't meet the demand, couldn't put out. There's no reason why I should ask you to feel this with me, and I won't blame you for avoiding it; I've done that myself. I always avoid extremes, even during sleep. Besides, we all recognize the burden of my dream: Life so diverse, the Grand Masquerade of Mortality shriveling to a hole in the ground. Still, that did not exhaust the sense of the dream, and the remainder is essential to the interpretation of what I've set down about Fonstein, Sorella, or Billy even. I couldn't otherwise have described it. It isn't so much a dream as a communication. I was being shown—and I was aware of this in sleep—that I had made a mistake, a lifelong mistake: something wrong, false, now fully manifest.

Revelations in old age can shatter everything you've put in place from the beginning—all the wiliness of a lifetime of expertise and labor, interpreting and reinterpreting in patching your fortified delusions, the work of the swarm of your defensive shock troops, which will go on throwing up more perverse (or insane) barriers. All this is bypassed in a dream like this one. When you have one of these, all you can do is bow to the inevitable conclusions.

Your imagination of strength is connected to your apprehensions of brutality, where that brutality is fully manifested or absolute. Mine is a New World version of reality—granting me the presumption that there is anything real about it. In the New World, your strength *doesn't* give out. That was the reason why your European parents, your old people, fed you so well in this land of youth. They were trained in submission, but you were free and bred in liberty. You were equal, you were strong, and here you could not be put to death, as Jews *there* had been.

But your soul brought the truth to you so forcibly that you woke up in your fifty-fifty bed—half Jewish, half Wasp—since, thanks to the powers of memory, you were the owner of a Philadelphia mansion (too disproportionate a reward), and there the dream had just come to a stop. An old man resuming ordinary consciousness opened his still-frightened eyes and saw the bronze brier-bush lamp with bulbs glowing in it. His neck on two pillows, stacked for reading, was curved like a shepherd's crook.

It wasn't the dream alone that was so frightful, though that was bad enough; it was the accompanying revelation that was so hard to take. It wasn't death that had scared me, it was disclosure: I wasn't what I thought I was. I really didn't understand merciless brutality. And whom should I take this up with now? Deirdre was gone; I can't discuss things like this with my son—he's all administrator and executive. That left Fonstein and Sorella. Perhaps.

Sorella had said, I recall, that Fonstein, in his orthopedic boot, couldn't vault over walls and escape like Douglas Fairbanks. In the movies, Douglas Fairbanks was always too much for his enemies. They couldn't hold him. In *The Black Pirate* he disabled a sailing vessel all by himself. Holding a knife, he slid down the mainsail, slicing it in half. You couldn't have locked a man like that in a cattle car; he would have broken out. Sorella wasn't speaking of Douglas Fairbanks, nor did she refer to Fonstein only. Her remark was ultimately meant for me. Yes, she was talking of me and also of Billy Rose. For Fonstein was Fonstein—he was Mitteleuropa. I, on the other hand, was from the Eastern Seaboard—born in New Jersey, educated at Washington Square College, a big mnemonic success in Philadelphia. I was a Jew of an entirely different breed. And therefore (yes, go on, you can't avoid it now) closer to Billy Rose and his rescue operation, the personal underground inspired by *The Scarlet Pimpernel*—the Hollywood of Leslie Howard, who acted the Pimpernel, substituted for the Hollywood of Douglas Fairbanks. There was no way, therefore, in which I could grasp the real facts in the case of Fonstein. I hadn't understood *Fonstein* v. *Rose,* and I badly wanted to say this to Harry and Sorella. You pay a price for being a child of the New World.

I decided to switch off the lamp, which, fleetingly, was associated with the thicket in which Abraham-*avinu* had found a ram caught by the horns—as you see, I was bombarded from too many sides. Now illuminated particles of Jewish history were coming at me.

An old man has had a lifetime to learn to control his jitters in the night. Whatever I was (and that, at this late stage, still remained to be seen), I would need strength

89

in the morning to continue my investigation. So I had to take measures to avoid a fretful night. Great souls may welcome insomnia and are happy to think of God or Science in the dead of night, but I was too disturbed to think straight. An important teaching of the Mnemosyne System, however, is to learn to make your mind a blank. You will yourself to think nothing. You expel all the distractions. Tonight's distractions happened to be very serious. I had discovered for how long I had shielded myself from unbearable imaginations—no, not imaginations, but recognitions—of murder, of relish in torture, of the ground bass of brutality, without which no human music ever is performed.

So I applied my famous method. I willed myself to think nothing. I shut out all thoughts. When you think nothing, consciousness is driven out. Consciousness being gone, you are asleep.

I conked out. It was a mercy.

In the morning, I found myself being supernormal. At the bathroom sink I rinsed my mouth, for it was parched (the elderly often suffer from such dryness). Shaved and brushed, I exercised on my ski machine (mustn't let the muscles go slack) and then I dressed and, when dressed, stuck my shoes under the revolving brush. Once more in rightful possession of a fine house, where Francis X. Biddle was once a neighbor and Emily Dickinson a guest at tea (there were other personages to list), I went down to breakfast. My housekeeper came from the kitchen with granola, strawberries, and black coffee. First the coffee, more than the usual morning fix.

"How did you sleep?" said Sarah, my old-fashioned caretaker. So much discretion, discernment, wisdom of life rolled up in this portly black lady. We didn't communicate in words, but we tacitly exchanged information at a fairly advanced level. From the amount of coffee I swallowed she could tell that I was shamming supernormalcy. From my side, I was aware that possibly I was crediting Sarah with very wide powers because I missed my wife, missed contact with womanly intelligence. I recognized also that I had begun to place my hopes and needs on Sorella Fonstein, whom I now was longing to see. My mind persisted in placing the Fonsteins in Sarasota, in winter quarters with the descendants of Hannibal's elephants, amid palm trees and hibiscus. An idealized Sarasota, where my heart apparently was yearning ever.

Sarah put more coffee before me in my study. Probably new lines had appeared in my face overnight—signs indicating the demolition of a long-standing structure. (How *could* I have been such a creep!)

At last my Fonstein call was answered—I was phoning on the half hour.

A young man spoke. "Hello, who is this?"

How clever of Swerdlow to suggest trying the old listed number.

"Is this the Fonstein residence?"

"That's what it is."

"Would you be Gilbert Fonstein, the son?"

"I would not," the young person said, breezy but amiable. He was, as they say, laid back. No suggestion that I was deranging him (Sorella entered into this—

she liked to make bilingual puns). "I'm a friend of Gilbert's, house-sitting here. Walk the dog, water the plants, set the timed lights. And who are you?"

"An old relative—friend of the family. I see that I'll have to leave a message. Tell them that it has to do with another Fonstein who lives in Jerusalem and claims to be an uncle or cousin to Harry. I had a call from a rabbi—X/Y—who feels that something should be done, since the old guy is off the wall."

"In what way?"

"He's eccentric, deteriorated, prophetic, psychopathic. A decaying old man, but he's still ebullient and full of protest. . . ."

I paused briefly. You never can tell whom you're talking to, seen or unseen. What's more, I am one of those suggestible types, apt to take my cue from the other fellow and fall into his style of speech. I detected a certain freewheeling charm in the boy at the other end, and there was an exchange of charm for charm. Evidently I wanted to engage this young fellow's interest. In short, to imitate, to hit it off and get facts from him.

"This old Jerusalem character says he's a Fonstein and wants money?" he said. "You sound as if you yourself were in a position to help, so why not wire money."

"True. However, Harry could identify him, check his credentials, and naturally would want to hear that he's turned up alive. He may have been on the dead list. Are you only a house-sitter? You sound like a friend of the family."

"I see we're going to have a talk. Hold a minute while I find my bandanna. It's starting to be allergy time, and

92

my whole head is raw. . . . Which relative are you?"

"I run an institute in Philadelphia."

"Oh, the memory man. I've heard of you. You go back to the time of Billy Rose—*that* flake. Harry disliked talking about it, but Sorella and Gilbert often did. . . . Can you hold on till I locate the handkerchief? Wiping my beard with Kleenex leaves crumbs of paper."

When he laid down the phone, I used the pause to place him plausibly. I formed an image of a heavy young man—a thick head of hair, a beer paunch, a T-shirt with a logo or slogan. *Act Up* was now a popular one. I pictured a representative member of the youth population seen on every street in every section of the country and even in the smallest of towns. Rough boots, stone-washed jeans, bristly cheeks—something like Leadville or Silverado miners of the last century, except that these young people were not laboring, never would labor with picks. It must have diverted him to chat me up. An old gent in Philadelphia, moderately famous and worth lots of money. He couldn't have imagined the mansion, the splendid room where I sat holding the French phone, expensively rewired, an instrument once the property of a descendant of the Merovingian nobility. (I wouldn't give up on the Baron Charlus.)

The young man was not a hang-loose, hippie handyman untroubled by intelligence, whatever else. I was certain of that. He had much to tell me. Whether he was malicious I had no way of saying. He was manipulative, however, and he had already succeeded in setting the tone of our exchange. Finally, he had information about the Fonsteins, and it was information I wanted.

"I do go back a long way," I said. "I've been out of touch with the Fonsteins for too many years. How have they arranged their retirement? Do they divide their year between New Jersey and a warm climate? Somehow I fancy them in Sarasota."

"You need a new astrologer."

He wasn't being satirical—protective rather. He now treated me like a senior citizen. He gentled me.

"I was surprised lately when I reckoned up the dates and realized the Fonsteins and I last met about thirty years ago, in Jerusalem. But emotionally I was in contact—that does happen." I tried to persuade him, and I felt in reality that it was true.

Curiously, he agreed. "It would make a dissertation subject," he said. "Out of sight isn't necessarily out of mind. People withdraw into themselves, and then they work up imaginary affections. It's a common American condition."

"Because of the continental U.S.A.—the terrific distances?"

"Pennsylvania and New Jersey are neighboring states."

"I do seem to have closed out New Jersey mentally," I admitted. "You sound as though you have studied . . . ?"

"Gilbert and I were at school together."

"Didn't he do physics at Cal Tech?"

"He switched to mathematics—probability theory."

"There I'm totally ignorant."

"That makes two of us," he said, adding, "I find you kind of interesting to talk to."

"One is always looking for someone to have a real exchange with."

He seemed to agree. He said, "I'm inclined to make the time for it, whenever possible."

He had described himself as a house-sitter, without mentioning another occupation. In a sense I was a house-sitter myself, notwithstanding that I owned the property. My son and his wife may also have seen me in such a light. A nice corollary was that my soul played the role of sitter in my body.

It did in fact cross my mind that the young man wasn't altogether disinterested. That I was undergoing an examination or evaluation. So far, he had told me nothing about the Fonsteins except that they didn't winter in Sarasota and that Gilbert had studied mathematics. He didn't say that he himself had attended Cal Tech. And when he said that out of sight wasn't invariably out of mind, I thought his dissertation, if he had written one, might have been in the field of psychology or sociology.

I recognized that I was half afraid of asking direct questions about the Fonsteins. By neglecting them, I had compromised my right to ask freely. There were things I did and did not want to hear. The house-sitter sensed this, it amused him, and he led me on. He was light and made sporty talk, but I began to feel there was a grim side to him.

I decided that it was time to speak up, and I said, "Where can I reach Harry and Sorella, or is there a reason you can't give out their number?"

"I haven't got one."

"Please don't talk riddles."

"They can't be reached."

"What are you telling me! Did I put it off too long?"

"I'm afraid so."

"They're dead, then."

I was shocked. Something essential in me caved in, broke down. At my age, a man is well prepared to hear news of death. What I felt most sharply and immediately was that I had abandoned two extraordinary people whom I had always said I valued and held dear. I found myself making a list of names: Billy is dead; Mrs. Hamet, dead; Sorella, dead; Harry, dead. All the principals, dead.

"Were they sick? Did Sorella have cancer?"

"They died about six months ago, on the Jersey Turnpike. The way it's told, a truck and trailer went out of control. But I wish I didn't have to tell you this, sir. As a relative, you'll take it hard. They were killed instantly. And thank God, because their car folded on them and it took welders to cut the bodies free— This must be hard for somebody who knew them well."

He was, incidentally, giving me the business. To some extent, I had it coming. But at any moment during these thirty years, any of us might have died in an instant. I too might have. And he was wrong to assume that I was a Jew of the old type, bound to react sentimentally to such news as this.

"You *are* a senior citizen, you said. You'd have to be, given the numbers."

My voice was low. I said I was one. "Where were the Fonsteins going?"

"They were driving from New York, bound for Atlantic City."

I saw the bloodstained bodies delivered from the car and stretched out on the grass slope—the police flares, the crush of diverted traffic and the wavering of the dark, gassed atmosphere, the sucking shrieks of the ambulance, the paramedics and their body bags. Last summer's heat was tormenting. You might say the dead sweated blood.

If you're deciding which is the gloomiest expressway in the country, the Jersey Pike is certainly a front runner. This was no place for Sorella, who loved Europe, to be killed. Harry's forty American years of compensation for the destruction of his family in Poland suddenly were up.

"Why were they going to Atlantic City?"

"Their son was there, having trouble."

"Was he gambling?"

"It was pretty widely known, so I'm able to say. After all, he wrote a mathematical study on winning at blackjack. Math mavens say it's quite a piece of work. On the real-life side, he's gotten into trouble over this."

They were rushing to the aid of their American son when they were killed.

"It must be very dreary to hear this," the young man said.

"I looked forward to seeing them again. I'd been promising myself to resume contact."

"I don't suppose death is the worst . . . ," he said.

I wasn't about to go into eschatology with this kid on the telephone and start delineating the various grades of evil. Although, God knows, the phone may encourage many forms of disclosure, and you may hear as much if not more from the soul by long distance as face to face.

"Which one was driving?"

"Mrs. Fonstein was, and maybe being reckless."

"I see—an emergency, and a mother in a terrible hurry. Was she still huge?"

"The same for years, and right up against the wheel. But there weren't many people like Sorella Fonstein. You don't want to criticize."

"I'm not criticizing," I said. "I would have gone to the funeral to pay my respects."

"Too bad you didn't come and speak. It wasn't much of a memorial service."

"I might have told the Billy Rose story to a gathering of friends in the chapel."

"There was no gathering," the young man said. "And did you know that when Billy died, they say that he couldn't be buried for a long time. He had to wait until the court decided what to do about the million-dollar tomb provision in his will. There was a legal battle over it."

"I never heard."

"Because you don't read the *News*, or *Newsday*. Not even the *Post*."

"Was *that* what happened!"

"He was kept on ice. This used to be discussed by

98

the Fonsteins. They wondered about the Jewish burial rules."

"Does Gilbert take any interest in his Jewish background—for instance, in his father's history?"

Gilbert's friend hesitated ever so slightly—just enough to make me think that he was Jewish himself. I don't say that he disowned being a Jew. Evidently he didn't want to reckon with it. The only life he cared to lead was that of an American. So hugely absorbing, that. So absorbing that one existence was too little for it. It could drink up a hundred existences, if you had them to offer, and reach out for more.

"What you just asked is—I translate—whether Gilbert is one of those science freaks with minimal human motivation," he said. "You have to remember what a big thing gambling is to him. It never could be my thing. You couldn't pay me to go to Atlantic City, especially since the double-deck disaster. They put a double-deck bus on the road, filled with passengers bound for the casino. It was too high to clear one of the viaducts, and the top was torn away."

"Did many die? Were heads sheared off?"

"You'd have to check the *Times* to find out."

"I wouldn't care to. But where is Gilbert now? He inherited, I suppose."

"Well, sure he did, and right now he's in Las Vegas. He took a young lady with him. She's trained in his method, which involves memorizing the deck in every deal. You keep mental lists of cards that have been played, and you apply various probability factors. They tell me that the math of it is just genius."

"The system depends on memorizing?"

"Yes. That's up your alley. Is Gilbert the girl's lover? is the next consideration. Well, this wouldn't work without sex interest. The gambling alone wouldn't hold a young woman for long. Does she enjoy Las Vegas? How could she not? It's the biggest showplace in the world—the heart of the American entertainment industry. Which city today is closest to a holy city—like Lhasa or Calcutta or Chartres or Jerusalem? Here it could be New York for money, Washington for power, or Las Vegas attracting people by the millions. Nothing to compare with it in the history of the whole world."

"Ah," I said. "It's more in the Billy Rose vein than in the Harry Fonstein vein. But how is Gilbert making out?"

"I haven't finished talking about the sex yet," said the bitter-witty young man. "Is the gambling a turn-on for sex, or does sex fuel the gambling? Figuring it as a sublimation. Let's assume that for Gilbert, abstraction is dominant. But past a certain abstraction point, people are said to be definitely mad."

"Poor Sorella—poor Harry! Maybe it was their death that threw him."

"I can't make myself responsible for a diagnosis. My own narcissistic problem is plenty severe. I confess I expected a token legacy, because I was damn near a family member and looked after Gilbert."

"I see."

"You don't see. This brings my faith in feelings face to face with the real conditions of existence."

"Your feelings for Fonstein and Sorella?"

"The feelings Sorella led me to believe she had for me."

"Counting on you to take care of Gilbert."

"Well . . . this has been a neat conversation. Good to talk to a person from the past who was so fond of the Fonsteins. We'll all miss them. Harry had the dignity, but Sorella had the dynamism. I can see why you'd be upset—your timing was off. But don't pine too much."

On this commiseration, I cradled the phone, and there it was, on its high mount, a conversation piece from another epoch sitting before a man with an acute need for conversation. Stung by the words of the house-sitter. I also considered that owing to Gilbert, the Fonsteins from their side had avoided me—he was so promising, the prodigy they had had the marvelous luck to produce and who for mysterious reasons (Fonstein would have felt them to be mysterious American reasons) had gone awry. They wouldn't have wanted me to know about this.

As for pining—well, that young man had been putting me on. He was one of those lesser devils that come out of every pore of society. All you have to do is press the social soil. He was taunting me—for my Jewish sentiments. Dear, dear! Two more old friends gone, just when I was ready after thirty years of silence to open my arms to them: Let's sit down together and recall the past and speak again of Billy Rose—"sad stories of the death of kings." And the "sitter" had been putting it to me, existentialist style. Like: Whose disappearance will fill you with despair, sir? Whom can you not live without? Whom do you painfully long for? Which of your dead hangs over you daily? Show me where and how death has mutilated you. Where are your wounds? Whom would you pursue beyond the gates of death?

What a young moron! Doesn't he think I know all that?

I had a good mind to phone the boy back and call him on his low-grade cheap-shot nihilism. But it would be an absurd thing to do if improvement of the understanding (his understanding) was my aim. You can never dismantle all these modern mental structures. There are so many of them that they face you like an interminable vast city.

Suppose I were to talk to him about the roots of memory in feeling—about the themes that collect and hold the memory; if I were to tell him what retention of the past really means. Things like: "If sleep is forgetting, forgetting is also sleep, and sleep is to consciousness what death is to life. So that the Jews ask even God to remember, 'Yiskor Elohim.' "

God doesn't forget, but your prayer requests him particularly to remember your dead. But how was I to make an impression on a kid like that? I chose instead to record everything I could remember of the Bellarosa Connection, and set it all down with a Mnemosyne flourish.